MANIACS
THE KRITTIKA CONFLICT

NICK S. THOMAS

ISBN 978-1-909149-16-8

Typeset by Swordworks Books
Printed and bound in the UK & US
A catalogue record of this book is available
from the British Library

Cover design by Swordworks Books
www.swordworks.co.uk

MANIACS
THE KRITTIKA CONFLICT

NICK S. THOMAS

CHAPTER ONE

Sharini II, Deneb System.
FROM THE WIKIWORLD ENTRY -
A former mining colony now occupied by smugglers, thieves, and others who have fled or been banished from worlds of The Alliance of Free Worlds, and the United Systems of VASI. Inhabitants exhibit no allegiance to either side of the war and are typically hostile to all. WARNING FROM THE INTERPLANETARY PEACEKEEPING AGENCY (IPA) - avoid any travel to or within the system.

"We've got another one, boys!"

"Hell, yeah!"

"Wohoo!"

The three triumphant scumbags traipsed past the cellblocks with arrogant swaggers and greasy smiles. One hit the bars of the cell door with the stock of his rifle. The girl inside winced on every impact. Her pain and suffering only brought further pleasure to her captors. She was just fifteen years old and had never experienced how harsh life could be until a few days before. Several more thugs cheered at the sight of their latest haul.

Two of the goons dragged a body along, a woman who couldn't be much older than twenty. Blood dripped from her forehead where she had been knocked unconscious, but she was beginning to regain composure. Her vision was still blurred, but she could tell by her surroundings that they were a long way from civilization. Her head was dropped as she was being hauled along over the shoulders of two of the stinking excuses for human beings.

The tips of her shoes were digging trenches in the dirt and grime of the floor. Some of it looked like dried blood that had been there for years. She could smell the salty and putrid smell of her captors' sweat. It was only overpowered by the disgusting smell of whatever they had cooking in a far off room. They passed the first girl's cell and reached the next. She was thrown inside like a ragdoll. Her instincts and muscle memory did all they could do to breakfall safely onto the hard metal floor. She saved herself from any injury, but it still hurt like hell as she rolled onto her face.

"Who'd you think she is?" asked one.

"Fuck knows, someone with money, or with a rich mommy and daddy at least. Someone who'll care enough

6

to cough up whatever we want."

"Shame, she'd be a real treat for the lads."

"You know the rules. Nobody touches the girls while there's any chance we'll get paid for 'em."

He grunted and walked off in disappointment. The other two looked down at the body of the girl. She was average height, slim and athletically built. Blond curly hair was tied back, but it was clear she normally spent plenty of time on it. She wore close fitting combat trousers, tall matching boots, a khaki blouse, and tan leather body warmer. She had the look of a woman trying to dress down, but the individual cost and cut of every item she wore betrayed her intentions.

"Posh girl, aren't ya? Well we have seen plenty come and go through here. You better hope someone cares enough to pay for you, or you'll be next week's entertainment!"

They slammed the door shut, and a booming echo pulsed through her ears, straining her already aching head. Gone was the stinking smell of old sweat, replaced by the putrid smell of urine and damp. She felt like hurling, but coughed up blood instead.

"Are you okay?" came a faint voice.

It was the first friendly voice she'd heard all day and staggered to her feet. It was coming from the other cell they had passed on the way in. She grasped the bars of the cell door to support her and replied, "What is this place?"

"Hell."

"What?"

"Where you stay till somebody pays your ransom, or anyone else pays enough to have you for themselves."

She shook her head in disbelief.

"What's your name?"

The older girl hesitated for a moment, as she tried to make sense of it all despite her pounding headache. She was about to reply with her name when she reconsidered her answer for a second before finally answering.

"Erin, you?"

"Skylar...Gutierrez."

Erin knew the name immediately.

"The Gutierrez Corporation, your his daughter? Sure you want to be throwing that name around here?"

"It's the only thing that'll keep me alive and...untouched. My father will come for me. Is there anyone coming for you?"

She was silent as she thought about it for a moment. In theory there would be, but she had to be very careful about revealing her identity.

I'm a long way from home, and it's anyone's guess what they'll do if they find out who I am, she thought but didn't say.

"I hope so," she replied.

Screams rang out from down the corridor, and the two girls clung to the doors to try and see the cause of it. The painful cries were getting louder until one of the kidnappers passed them. He was pulling a girl down the corridor by her hair. He stopped at Erin's door.

"This one's daddy didn't feel like paying up. That's okay, more perks to this job than just the cash!" he yelled, breaking out into a horrible laugh as he carried on down the corridor.

* * *

"This is my last gig, so let's do this right," said Carter across the radio.

He looked over to the other vehicle and to his soon to be successor Mason who stood atop it. Mason nodded in acknowledgement as he turned back to the heavy calibre machine gun and slid the safety off. It was 1300 hours, and they were racing across open terrain in the clear light of day. The surface was a dusty wasteland, and the sun beat down hard without any cloud cover to save them from the fiery rays.

Mason was in his mid-thirties and was of average height but of strong build. He wore tan combat trousers and black body armour that was so dusty and faded it almost blended into the dusky landscape. A moisture wicking shirt ended at his elbows, revealing his muscular forearms. On his head was a compact and close fitting helmet, and slim line goggles kept the debris from his eyes. His armour was adorned with so many magazines of ammunition and grenades it looked like he was set for war, not a rescue operation.

A combat knife was suspended upside down on the chest of his armour ready for quick release, and a long barrelled pistol holstered on his thigh. Every part of his equipment was well worn and heavily used. He knelt forward to speak to the driver.

"Hell of a day for it!"

Ben Liu was at the wheel and wiped is sleeve around his mouth to soak up the sweat as he agreed.

"Why would anyone choose to live here?"

The metal armoured plates of the vehicle were hot enough to cook on, and their destination up ahead was a hazy blur. Mason looked over to see Josiah and Peter were standing patiently in the other vehicle, with their weapons at the ready as if they didn't even notice the heat that made the air so thick. The two old timers had been there since the beginning. He looked back and could see the target was now in sight.

The core of the kidnappers' base was a large freight vessel that had been long abandoned. It had expanded to become a small town for the low life scum who chose to dwell there. Mason had studied the surveillance images for hours on end, and he felt like he had lived there among them. It was rare they were able to carry out such a noble mission, so he wanted to do it right.

"Feels good to be doing a good thing, doesn't it, Liu?"

"A missing kid in the hands of scum like this? It was

always my worst nightmare."

He could tell Liu took it to heart more than any of them. His old detective training and experience reminding him of kidnappings he'd worked in the past. They could see the sentries at the edge of the smuggler town, but the dust their vehicles were kicking up was hiding their true firepower and intentions.

Here we go, he thought to himself.

A five metre ramshackle wall surrounded the town and seamlessly joined onto the hull of the old freighter. Two watch towers rose up from behind the walls, and they could already see a hive of activity from those stationed on them. Mason turned the gun around on its mounts and took quick aim at the tower. He turned one last time to look at the Boss, Carter, who merely gave him the nod to give the green light.

Mason was the first to pull the trigger. Killing low life scum gave him little pause for thought. The heavy weapons opened up on both vehicles as they got within a hundred metres of the walls. The laser weapons pulsated so loudly as they fired it was almost deafening. The vibrations could be felt through the frames of the trucks when the towers at the gate exploded almost in sequence, and they could hear the screams and shouts of panic as the debris smashed to the ground either side of the walls.

At just fifty metres from the tall gates the two guns were turned on the entrance and riddled it with fire, but they did not slow down. The large steel bumpers, reinforced by bars running the length of the chassis, smashed into the weakened structure. The impact barely slowed the two trucks as they burst through the entrance. Just a few lasers zipped past as they steamed in, but the relentless gunfire from the fire breathing trucks did not slow either.

Mason's vehicle was in the lead, and he quickly caught sight of the second defensive line that he recognised instantly. It was an anti aircraft quad laser. It looked almost a hundred years old but no less effective than it ever was. As he swivelled the gun around to bring his target to bear, a cry of panic came from Liu.

"Take it out!"

The quad gun spun quickly to lock onto their truck and got off the first few shots before Mason could fire. The first hit the thickened ram front of the vehicle and was absorbed but shunted them violently off course. The second shot skimmed the upper framework half a metre from Mason's head, and he felt the burn singe the stubble on his chin. He barely managed to keep a grip on the weapon, squeezing the trigger before they were vaporised by the onslaught.

The lasers hit the thin metal shield that was protection against debris and fragmentation only. Mason's fire punctured through with no resistance, cutting the quad gun in half. The top section flew off and hit a parked vehicle, crushing one of the kidnappers; what remained was a twisted wreck.

"Fuck, yeah!" yelled Mason.

Liu breathed a sigh of relief, realising they had come within a split second of instant death. Lasers rushed past their flank as Carter's vehicle kept up the assault. They had lost only a little of their momentum, and the two guns continued raining down fire on the base. Incongruous characters were crawling out from every hole, to be cut down by the relentless heavy guns.

Mason spun the gun around to spray the flanks racing for the entrance of the old freighter.

"Hold on!" Liu shouted.

He turned as they hit the ramp. It had just enough headroom for the vehicle to fit through, but not with him standing up. He ducked under in time and took a deep breath. He'd almost forgotten and came close to losing his head. The vehicle was at the top of the ramp in seconds and smashed into tables and chairs, in what was a makeshift dining and gambling area.

The two trucks slid to a halt; the wheels locking under the pressure of the braking. As they stopped, one of the kidnappers jumped on one and put a pistol through the side of the driver's hatch, but Liu opened the door and kicked it hard. The heavy metal plate smashed into the guy's stomach, forcing him to keel over. His gun fired up into the ceiling.

Liu leapt from the truck and onto the lowly goon

before he could recover. He launched forward with a knee into the head. The man flew back against a nearby table, cracking his back over it. Liu continued forward with no mercy. He took hold of the pistol hand and struck the inner elbow with a knife hand. The gun arced around into the goon's face.

"No, no!" he screamed in fear.

Liu forced the man's own finger back on the trigger, and a laser struck him dead in the face, killing him instantly. Mason jumped from the truck in time to see the brutality from his colleague. It was nothing new in his line of work, but it was coming from the former detective. He could see in his face that the situation really got to his friend.

"Go!" Carter ordered.

The other team was already past them and heading for the starboard corridor. Liu reached over to his rifle, which was slung on the side of the dusty truck, and quickly followed Mason to the port side. Cries of panic echoed down the corridor. Three gang members rushing towards the sounds of chaos quickly met them, but they were ill prepared for what was hitting them.

Mason and Liu were at a jogging pace, descending on them with their rifles firmly set in the shoulder, and firing before their opponents could even lift the pistols from their sides. The shots took the thugs off their feet and planted them firmly on the deck of the old ship, but Mason did not stop. The two ran over the bloodied bodies without breaking stride. The faint smell of burning flesh crept into Mason's nostrils as he passed the bodies. It was a putrid and disgusting odour that had become so familiar to him he could ignore it. If anything, it reassured him that his shots had met their targets.

"Another twenty metres and swing a right," said Liu.

He reached the turning up ahead and slid to a halt in shock. Liu saw the glow of high power lasers light up the corridor they were entering and spotted Mason's hesitation. He grabbed the back of his body armour, hauling him back as a flurry of laser fire flashed past. Mason took a deep breath.

"Second hurdle," he stated.

Liu nodded.

"Carter's behind schedule."

"Carter, where the fuck are you?" Mason shouted through the comms.

Gunfire followed as the response came through.

"Dealing with some shit, hang on!" yelled Carter.

"That's nice," he said to Liu.

The fire let up for a second, and he took a quick peak around the corner but recoiled even quicker when another hail of laser fire screamed past his face. He lifted up his wrist to check the time.

"Fuck, come on, come on."

"We aren't going anywhere like this!"

As the last word came out, a large explosion rang out,

and several large pieces of the weapon that had been firing at them flew past the corridor entrance beside them.

"All right, that's it, go!"

They rushed out from the cover to find the corridor scattered with twisted metal and rubble. Two of the kidnappers lay dead near the side of the weapon, and Mason caught sight of Carter's team approaching from the other side.

"Cells are this way," he added, as they took a turn at the junction.

As Carter led the way past the wreckage, a huge blade flashed across, making him stop quickly. A hulking brute of a man flew past in front of him. The blade carved into the wall in front of them. Carter quickly responded with a knee into his gut, but the strike barely made the man flinch. He swung the blade around to cut at Carter's head. He ducked down, and the blade hit the far sidewall.

Mason looked for a shot, but it couldn't be made safely with the Boss between him and the thug. Carter lifted his rifle, but the man grabbed it by the barrel, ripping it from his hands, and delivering a brutal punch to his face with the blade still in his hands. The blow hit like a train and wobbled his legs. Mason caught him as he fell back and threw him forward towards the thug.

The clumsy kidnapper took a hard swing that Carter ducked under and passed by. It was Mason's turn to weigh in, and he did so without hesitation. He knew he couldn't risk a shot with the Boss on the other side, so he leapt forward and drew his knife from his chest. His rifle dropped down to his side as their attacker came at him. He reached forward with his offhand to parry the blade at the wrist wielding it. His arm almost buckled under the strength of attack, but he held as he thrust his blade into the man's neck.

The blade seemingly missed the windpipe of the thug's thick neck, but it caused enough pain for him to drop his machete-like cleaver. Mason grabbed his rifle and smashed the stock into his face. He stumbled back against the sidewall. The thug grabbed the knife in an attempt to draw it out. Mason was impressed with his resolve and toughness, but was no less inclined to spare his life.

A burst of laser fire rang out from the Boss. The man was dead. Mason looked over to see Carter breathe a sigh of relief as blood trickled from his mouth.

"Getting too old for this shit," he muttered.

"Yeah, you are," replied Mason.

"Your vote of confidence is overwhelming," Carter grunted.

"Sure is good to have friends."

Mason carried on at the lead. They reached the cellblocks and found no resistance at all. Everyone guarding it had already been dealt with, but they knew the scene outside would be wholly different. The body of a girl lay on the floor at the entrance to the cellblocks. She had a laser burn on the side of her head.

"That's fresh," said Peter.

"Not good," added Liu.

"Skylar Gutierrez? Skylar Gutierrez!" Mason called.

"Here!" a desperate cry rang out.

He rushed to the quivering voice and looked through the bars. The terrified girl was seemingly unharmed.

"I'm Max Mason. We've been hired to get you out of here."

"Hired? You're not the Army?"

"No, Ma'am, not even close. Stand back."

She looked completely stunned but did as he asked.

"Come on, Mason, we gotta get the hell out of here!" Josiah shouted.

Mason pulled out a magnetic explosive device from his webbing and slapped it onto the lock. He turned away, and the small shaped charge popped and blew the lock off with little effort. He grabbed the bars and ripped the door open. The girl was quivering at the back of the cell and clearly wasn't sure whether to trust them or not.

"Who sent you?"

"Your father hired us to get you out of this hell hole."

"Prove it."

"Sorry, no time."

He stepped forward and grabbed her. She tried to resist but to no avail.

"Get off me!" she screamed.

He held her at arms reach, slapping her lightly on the face. It was more to shock than hurt her.

"Pull yourself together, or do you want us to leave you with these scum?"

She shook her head and submitted, knowing she was powerless to fight him even if she wanted to. She dipped her head and then looked back up as she remembered something important.

"Wait, there's another girl here."

"We passed her on the way in. She's gone."

"No, in the next cell. Please help her. I'll get my father to pay you for it."

Mason stopped and thought for a moment.

"What's the hold-up?" Josiah asked from the corridor.

"Check the cell beside us!"

He grabbed Skylar and hauled her out the cell while his comrades checked.

"There's a girl in there all right. She's gagged and tied to the bed," replied Josiah.

"Get her out."

"We ain't got all day."

"Do it!" yelled Liu.

The old timer turned to the short Asian with a scornful look.

"We aren't leaving her behind."

"And you think the target's daddy is gonna pay for god knows who?"

"We've already been paid to do this job. What more is it to us to take this one as well?"

"Get the girl!" Carter's voice boomed.

Josiah went silent. He would submit to the Boss' will, but he wouldn't do the job for Liu.

"We got incoming!"

Laser fire soared down the corridor.

"You've got ten seconds!" said Carter, taking up position to repel their attackers. Liu quickly put a charge on the locks, but it didn't completely break the seal.

"It's stuck!"

Mason rushed to his aid and grabbed hold of the bars of the upper part of the door.

"Put your back into it!" yelled Liu.

They tried with all their strength but failed to open it.

"Stand back," said Mason, lifting his rifle.

"You could weld it shut with that."

"Maybe, but it's this way or nothing."

He fired a dozen shots into the lock and another dozen into the hinges of the thick reinforced door.

"Now pull!"

The two of them grabbed the bars once again, heaving with everything they had until it prised open little more than twenty centimetres.

"That's all we're gonna get."

"It'll do."

"For you maybe," said Mason with a smile. "Only a girl

could fit through a gap like that."

Liu ripped off his body armour and webbing and squeezed into the cell.

"It's getting a little hot out here!" Carter shouted.

Mason looked back to see the Boss ducking for cover from gunfire which was rapidly growing nearer. The previously tied up woman was now on her feet. He was surprised to see she was not at all shaken like Skylar. She could clearly handle herself and was making a break for the door to join them.

"Name's Mason."

"Erin."

"You better hope we get paid up for this one!" Josiah called out.

Mason shook his head as Liu got out from the cell behind her and grabbed his gear.

"We're outta here!" cried Mason.

Carter was quick to his feet and running past the cells to lead the way. Peter and Josiah were providing fire to cover them as they made their way further inside the old freighter.

"Where are we going?" Erin asked.

Mason could tell she knew they were going deeper inside the ship, and it rightfully worried her.

"Just keep up and you'll be fine!"

She wasn't happy at having her question ignored, but he had no time to be concerned about anything but the plan.

"Come on, go!" Carter ordered.

He ushered them through a doorway, waiting with his rifle while they all rushed past him. As Josiah made it to the door, he caught sight of one of the kidnappers. He fired two shots with his rifle and punched the door release switch. He glanced back and saw a laser go through before the door sealed. It hit Josiah in the back.

His old friend was thrown of his feet and landed face first on the deck. Carter rushed to his side, but he was still breathing. He checked his back.

"One lucky son of a bitch, Joe."

"Yeah, your turn to get shot next time."

"No chance. We finish up here, and I'm done with this game for good," he said, groaning as he helped his friend to his feet.

"Where are you leading us?" pleaded Skylar.

"The hell out of here," Mason replied.

"But the exit is the other way," Erin added.

"No, the entrance is the other way, and it's now crawling with low life scum, all who want a piece of you."

"Climb in," said Carter.

Erin looked around to see the team was climbing into an escape module.

"That surely can't still work?"

"Bet your sweet little ass," Mason answered.

"The scum running this place keep it operational to escape in the event of the authorities ever bearing down on 'em."

"And it'll work in this atmosphere?"

"You sure do talk a lot," Mason muttered. He pushed her through the hatch where she tumbled, breaking her fall but recovered quickly. It did not go unnoticed by Mason.

She sure is very different to the useless spoilt brats like Skylar.

The escape module was cramped, with six seats running down each side and facing each other. They were all familiar with the setup.

"Never thought I'd ever have to actually use one of these things," said Skylar with a whimper and a tear.

They each pulled down the restraint loops over their seats and heard the engine fire up automatically as the sensors detected all were aboard and squared away.

"Ready for this, Mason?" asked Carter.

"No."

"This better work," said Liu.

"We'll never know if it doesn't."

"Good to know!" yelled Mason. The engines reached full power, and the pod lurched and rocketed off from the freighter. The pod had launched them up and out at a forty-degree angle from the kidnappers' base. It was only a minute or two before the descent began, and they felt a chute open to slow it down.

Skylar was breathing heavily and close to having a panic attack. The smell of fresh sweat filled the pod, combined with the burning smell of Josiah's armour that was still running hot from the laser shot. Carter lifted his arm and tapped a few buttons on a pad attached to his forearm.

"Our ride is on the way."

"We can't have got far?" asked Erin.

"Don't you worry, everything is in order," replied Carter.

"Didn't exactly go to plan. We're late, one more than planned, and I got shot," added Josiah.

"Life's a bitch."

Mason smiled. The two old friends bickered like an old couple, while Peter didn't say a word.

"Almost home now."

The pod came to a rough landing, and as doors released on impact, they felt the thick hot air flood in.

"Remind me not to take a holiday here," said Carter.

"Amen to that," Mason laughed.

They climbed out, and a small quadrotor flier floated up to their position, stopping a few metres away as Carter tapped a few more keys on the control pad. The vehicle had a two metre wide fan at each corner. It was completely open topped, without even a windshield. Two rows of Spartan seating and an open cargo bed lay behind the controls.

"You lot really travel in style," Erin said.

The ground erupted a few metres off, and dirt and dust were thrown over them. They could see a column of vehicles approaching.

"Get in!" Carter shouted.

"They must have known we were going for the pod," Mason said. They clambered aboard, and Skylar was tossed aboard in a rather undignified fashion.

"See what saving that other girl did!" screamed Josiah.

"Quit your bitching and shoot something!" Carter ordered.

Carter fired up the quadrotor and stormed forwards as the vehicles drew nearer.

"Hope you've got a damn good plan to get us out of this!"

Mason shook his head at Erin's lack of faith, lifted his rifle, and fired at the nearest truck approaching them.

"Mitchell, you better get your ass here now!" Mason hollered down the radio.

"Where the hell is he?" he muttered to himself.

"That junkie is gonna get us killed."

"You're just a bundle of laughs today, aren't you, Joe?" Mason jested.

Lasers pounded the ground around them, sending dust and debris up and over their heads.

"What are we doing, Boss?" Peter asked.

Just when he was out of ideas, a radio transmission came through.

"Mitchell here at the primary extraction. What is your status?"

"We need pickup now!"

"Move to secondary extraction?"

"Mitchell, we've got hostiles on our tail. Get your fucking ass to our coordinates now!"

The radio went silent for a few seconds, but the gunfire continued.

"Boss, you're running out of road. Two clicks, and you're facing a thousand metre cliff edge drop."

"What?" Mason yelled.

"We can't make that, not with this much weight," said Liu.

"Mitchell, you're gonna have to pick us up mid fall. Piggyback landing, you remember that?"

"What?" Josiah shouted.

"We don't have a choice."

"Boss, we ain't even tried it before," Mitchell added.

"Tough shit, do or die."

"This is one great rescue attempt," Erin said to Mason.

"Hey, not like there was anyone else coming for you. Count yourself lucky."

A laser struck Liu's arm, and he screamed out in pain. His rifle flew out his hands and overboard. Mason grabbed the back of his webbing. He was keeling dangerously over the edge and hauled him back in. The enemy vehicles were closing rapidly.

"Mitchell, where the hell are you?"

They could see the cliff edge now and the blur of the landscape way in the distance beyond it.

"What are you gonna do?"

"Go over the edge and hope for the best, Josiah," replied Carter.

"That's one hell of a leap of faith," said Peter.

"I'll take our chances on Mitchell over whatever those animals would do. Everyone hold on. This ain't gonna be pretty!"

The edge was a hundred metres away, and there was still no sign of Mitchell.

"Sure about this, Boss?"

"No, Mason!"

Mason could do nothing but smile.

Well, if it all fails, we won't live to know it.

"Here we go!"

They hit the edge, and the quadrotor soared from the cliff at such a speed, it felt as if they'd keep going forward. The skimmer could handle a few hundred metres, but not the sort of free fall they were about to begin. Just as the nose dipped, Mason looked back at the kidnappers' vehicles sliding to a halt at the edge. A thick dust cloud had been kicked up. A few lasers fired at them, but they were suddenly drowned out by the booming resonation of engines as a ship burst through the dust cloud and bearing down on them rapidly.

"There she is!"

Carter could see Mitchell descending rapidly to catch them, and he did everything he could to keep the nose up.

"Deploy the clamps!" he yelled.

Mason reached over and punched the switch that extended magnetic clamps from the body. They were intended for holding the vehicle down to a landing point, but it was their best shot at getting a safe landing. The transport ship soared beneath them as they reached five hundred metres from the craggy rocks below. The quadcopter landed hard on the top of the ship. They all jolted violently, and pain soared through their necks. They slid a few metres along the length of the fuselage until coming to a stop.

"We're on!" Carter called to Mitchell.

The nose began to lift, but they were still diving towards the rocks and an impending death.

"Mitchell, get us up! Mitchell!"

They had descended to only a hundred and fifty metres, and no one thought they were going to make it, when Mitchell fired the landing boosters and managed to gain some lift.

"Come on!" yelled Mason.

The nose lifted when they reached eighty metres, and they rushed forward over the desolate landscape before levelling off. Carter took in a deep breath of air in relief.

"Holy shit," he said in shock.

"Hell of a way to end a career, hey, Boss?" asked Mason.

"Not what I had in mind, but it'll do," he said with a smile.

CHAPTER TWO

"Welcome to the Foxy Lady," Mason said.

Erin turned to him with a painful look and smiled beneath gritted teeth.

"Really? The Foxy Lady?"

"Sure. She used to be named after the Boss' wife, but after his third marriage, he figured it was time for something more...universal."

"Classy."

"We thought so. She's a Leander class transport, top of the line twenty years ago, and still as solid as ever. Seen us through hell and back more than a few times."

"Looks homely," she said sarcastically.

"Sure is."

Her sarcasm had been wholly lost on Mason, who was never more pleased than when he returned to what was his home. The ramp closed behind them, and they began to lift off from the planet they'd all rather never see again in their lifetimes. Erin turned to see Skylar was being handed a cup of coffee from a crewmember she hadn't met. Skylar was still shaking and in shock. The fact Erin wasn't sparked Mason's curiosity. He led her over to Skylar and the other man who was in his mid-fifties. His hairline was receding, and he had a deeply weathered and wrinkled face. Despite this, he had a pleasant smile and the look of a trustworthy and friendly sort of fellow.

"This is Archibald Andrews, but we mostly called him Wizard. He's the ship's go to guy."

"Go to for what?"

"You want to have a good meal, stitch up a wound, or blow shit up, he's your man."

"That's quite a résumé."

"A what?" asked Mason.

"Nice to meet you," added Andrews. "I was told we'd only be having one guest."

"Yeah, this one was down there too. She'll be catching a ride with us."

"Until Gutierrez pays up," Josiah added.

"You've already met the merry one among the bunch. Josiah."

"Hey, I only want what is rightfully ours. We risked all our lives in there to get her out."

"And I am very thankful," replied Erin.

"Josiah likes his thanks in cash, and I can't say there

ain't one among us who doesn't share that thought," stated Mason.

Erin looked down at Skylar. She was still weeping.

"And helping a girl in need isn't enough?"

"Good will doesn't pay the bills," replied Mason.

She was taken aback.

It clearly hasn't occurred to her that money might be so much an issue.

"You've come from money then. Why's no one paid your ransom?"

"I...I was only taken yesterday. Nobody knows where I am."

"Trust me, those scum would have been more than keen to tell the world where you were if it meant some cash in hand. So why didn't you tell 'em?"

She went quiet, clearly not wanting to explain her circumstances.

"What are you, a runaway? Deserter? No, you can handle yourself, but you are no soldier. What have you got to hide?"

Andrews stood up and strode to her aid.

"Gentlemen, the girl's been through enough. Leave her be."

Mason backed down, but they all knew it would not be the end of it.

Carter strode into the room from the bridge.

"Well, now that's over, I'd like to personally welcome

you both aboard. I am Ed Carter, the Captain of this ship. We were hired by your father, Miss Gutierrez, and whom you will be returned to shortly. And you, we were not introduced?"

"Erin."

Carter was in his late sixties and clearly coming to the end of his chosen career. His hair was silky grey and short. He was tall and workmanlike in his appearance and walked with a stiffness in his left leg, which was inevitably a combat wound. He and Erin couldn't be from more different worlds, but she instantly felt as though she could trust him.

"Evidently, your manners haven't rubbed off on all your crew yet, Captain."

He smiled in response, which got a few laughs from those standing around.

"She thinks you're a charmer," Mason grinned.

"You've got no idea," he said with a smirk.

Carter turned to Skylar.

"We're en route to meet a representative of your father's. We rendezvous in about six hours. Until then, we will do our best to make you comfortable."

"A representative, my father won't be there?"

Mason shook his head. He wanted to rib the girl's father, but he turned to Erin and could see her shaking her head for him to back down. Something in the sincerity of her eyes made him do so.

"We're meeting his head of security, Arlon Thompson."

"Great."

"You have a problem with that?"

"Who cares?" added Josiah.

"Whatever, just get me there," she hissed.

"Gotta love the appreciation for us risking our lives," Josiah carried on.

"I thought you risked your lives for a payday," added Erin.

Josiah shot a glance over to the older girl, but she looked back defiantly. He wanted to take offence, but he wasn't ashamed of his mercenary ways.

"Any payday is a good day."

Erin sighed. She turned and looked to Liu who sat wincing in pain.

"You going to help him?" she asked Archibald.

"Yeah, just as soon as our guests are comfortable."

"Don't get paid if the goods aren't delivered on time and as expected," said Mason.

"That's what we are to you?"

"Today, yes," he replied and turned to Skylar.

"Your father really going to pay for your friend here?" She dipped her head to shy away from eye contact."

"Well?"

"I think so..." she whispered.

"Think!"

"Take it down a notch, Josiah. We've got a few hours

till the meet. Get some rest. This is my last job, so don't fight me," ordered Carter.

Josiah turned away and strode off, still fuming.

"Come on, I'll show you both to some fresh beds where you can get a little rest," said Archibald.

Skylar obliged and got to her feet with his help. He turned to see if Erin would join him.

"It's okay. I'm fine here."

"As you like it."

She looked around the room. It was the main cargo bay of the ship, but there were few commodities. Each side were the entrances to what must be the crew quarters. There were no names on the doors, only numbers. A small corridor at the far end from where they had entered seemed to lead to the bridge. A simple kitchen lay just before it. She guessed the table and chairs they were sitting around were the closest the ship came to a mess hall.

It was small for a transport ship, with a small payload, and surprisingly fast. The room was just three metres high, and mementos from a hundred worlds hung from the ceiling, flags, tapestries, models, and old pre-laser weapons. A police riot shield, and even the door to what looked like a bank vault was up there.

"I'm guessing you don't do a lot of commercial transport?" Erin asked.

"We do whatever jobs we can get. If that's moving something from A to B, we'll do it, but the kind of people who pay us to move stuff expect us to fight like hell to protect it. Not give up the goods at the first sign of trouble."

"Which side do you fight on?"

"Our own."

"Come on, you're soldiers. You must have some allegiance. The war's been going for what, six years, and you're telling me you're not involved?"

"Wars come and go. Life goes on. You know what the military pay you for putting your ass on the line for their cause?"

"And the pension policies suck," Liu added, smiling.

She looked over to him, still wincing in pain from his wound.

"Let me help you with that."

She walked over and helped him out of his armour. She reached for Wizard's med kit and pulled out a pair of scissors.

"You know what you're doing?" Mason asked.

"The basics, yeah."

She cut around his shirt and prised it from his skin. She was surprised to see a police tattoo on his upper arm. It was obvious that she recognised it.

"You are a Veni police officer?"

"Yeah, I was," he replied in a sad tone.

"And you aren't any longer?"

He looked up at her as if to ask if she was serious.

"I guess it's a long story of how you ended up here."

"It ain't that interesting. You're familiar with Veni?"

She hesitated for a moment. "I was there for a while some time ago."

"And anytime recently?" asked Mason.

"No," she replied. Her tone was sombre.

"We don't have much cause to ever go near a capital like Veni. We get plenty of jobs from there, but god forbid our employers would ever want us setting foot there," said Mason.

"So where are we meeting Mr Thompson?"

Her sudden subject change did not go unnoticed, but they were willing to entertain it.

"Luthien V, it's an IPA station. One of the only places we can safely meet him in the area. The girl's father is a key investor in USV worlds, and we're deep inside Alliance territory. God knows what she was doing out here in the first place. She'd be worth a fortune to any Alliance officials who knew she was here."

"We're in Alliance territory?" she asked with surprise.

"Sure are. The fact you didn't know that gets me curious. How did you end up in that cell?"

"I was on a research mission to a frontier world when our ship was attacked. That was the last thing I remember. But we were still in Vasi territory when that happened."

It sounded as if she was telling a half-truth.

"It's possible," added Liu. "Kidnappers working on

36

the border and taking Vasi civilians back within Alliance worlds. It would give them a layer of protection from official responses."

"Sounds like you're making shit up. There's been something not right about you since we found ya down there. But fuck it, what do I care? Another few hours, and you're a bonus for us in what was already a fine pay day."

"Nice to see I can bring some sunshine to your day," she snapped.

Mason smiled as he walked away and muttered, "Sunshine, hell I've had enough of that for one day too."

They were all tired, and most managed to get some sleep en route, but were glad to hear the Boss' voice over the intercom.

"Luthien V is up ahead, arrival in fifteen minutes. Have the girls ready for departure."

Mason stepped up to the deck to join the Boss who had become such a lifelong friend.

"This is it, you're really gonna call it a day here?"

"It's been a long time coming. My body ain't up to this work anymore. I've worked decades to amass enough money to retire to a good life. My luck can only go on so long. Time to get out and move on."

"Same here."

Josiah and Peter stepped into the room.

"All of you? You're going through with this?"

"We get paid what we're owed for this mission, and

I'm taking the cash back to the wife and gonna buy a Mk5 Dauntless. Travel the universe and make some money carrying goods as we do it."

"Somehow, I can't picture you living that life."

"It was always about the money. All this shooting and running, it's for you young guys."

"Peter?"

"Got a job lined up, security consultant on Themis II."

"Themis?"

"What of it?"

"Ain't gonna see a lot of action there."

"That's the point. No firearms allowed; lowest violent crime rate for twenty-five years running of any colony known to man. A quiet easy life."

"And you?" he asked the Boss.

"No idea. I figure I'll find a little peaceful world somewhere and kick my feet up."

"Sounds like you're all in for a barrel of laughs."

"Hey, I've had enough for a lifetime."

They turned back to the cockpit glass. Mitchell was coming in for his final descent to the station.

"Ever been here, Max?" asked Mitchell.

"No, you?"

"Yep. It was my last flight before I lost my licence."

"What licence?" asked a voice from behind them.

They all turned; Erin had made her way into the cabin.

"His commercial flight licence," Mason answered.

"Why?"

"Because he's a junky son of a bitch."

"Hey, fuck you, Josiah, who saved your ass this morning?"

"That's enough!" yelled Carter, pushing Josiah back. "He's needed to fly this thing, you're not. Another hour, and you'll never have to see each other again, so go and cool off."

He grunted and strode of angrily.

"It's true," said Mitchell. "I had some issues which I have since overcome. Been clean for two years. You can call me Felix."

"She ain't gonna be with us for much longer, so don't get too friendly."

"You're a cold mother, you know that, Max?"

Mason turned to Erin for some support, but she could not help but nod and agree, which brought a smile to Carter's face. Erin looked back, enjoying the moment with Felix. He was six foot, black, and of average build. His head was shaven, and he had a well-kept goatee and moustache. He looked to be in his mid-thirties and managed the controls while talking like a pro.

They felt the landing gear connect with the deck below. The landing pad immediately withdrew into a sealed hangar area where they could see people and vehicles going about their work. A greeting party of three people was waiting for them. They all wore perfectly cut and clean suits, which meant they could only be Arlon Thompson and his people.

Carter led the crew down the ramp with Skylar and Erin kept securely at the rear, until they were satisfied they were both safe and getting paid.

"I trust you were successful?" asked Arlon.

He couldn't see the girl because she was at the back of the crew.

"We got her out unharmed, yes. You have the final payment?"

"Let me see the girl."

Carter turned back and nodded for the crew to do so. He caught sight of her, but showed no emotion at all. They could also see that to him the girl was nothing more than a business transaction. He lifted a datapad from his pocket and tapped a few keys.

"One million credits deposited to your account. Please confirm."

Carter lifted his arm and looked at the display screen attached to his forearm. He already had his account open and smiled as he could see the money present and available.

"Before we finish up. We found another girl held in a cell next to Miss Gutierrez. She promised us her father would compensate us for our efforts in also rescuing her."

"Skylar, this girl, had you met her before your kidnap?"

She shook her head.

"Is she related to anyone you know back home?"

She responded the same.

"Then there is nothing I can do. This operation has already cost Mr Gutierrez substantially, both financially and his reputation amongst his business partners. Our business arrangement is as arranged and complete as soon as you transfer Miss Gutierrez to our custody."

"We risked our lives for this other girl!" Josiah protested loudly.

"And that was both your choice and now your problem."

Josiah went to speak, but Carter lifted his hand to stop him.

"Deal is a deal, Joe."

"Fuck sake," he muttered.

"I told them my father would help her," pleaded Skylar as she staggered towards Thompson.

"These fine men have rescued her, and she is now safe and free."

"Hey, Thompson?"

He looked up.

"You're a security chief, right?"

"Yes."

"Bet you're paid a damn fortune, and you haven't got a fucking clue what you're doing. Next time Gutierrez's daughter gets kidnapped, I'll be doubling our price to get her back, based on the fact it'll be your stupid fault," Mason spat.

The verbal assault and being looked at by the scornful

eyes of the crew took Arlon Thompson aback. He looked to Carter, as if to ask him to get his man under control, but the Boss only shook his head.

"Come on, let's go," he said to Skylar.

She turned back quickly to Erin. "I'm sorry."

"I'll be fine. You get along now."

Thompson led her away to their ship; a lavish luxury yacht they all knew would have cost more than any of them would likely earn in a lifetime.

"All money, no balls," said Josiah.

"Yep," replied Carter.

He turned and looked at the crew. "So, this is it."

Mason watched Mitchell lower several large crates from the cargo bay.

"You're leaving here and now?"

"I've got a ship waiting for me, and Josiah and Peter if they want to join me. I have been waiting to do this for too long. I wait another day, and there'll be another mission, and I'll never get out."

"There's no changing your mind?" asked Mason.

He shook his head.

"It's been a good run," Liu added.

"Max. Ship's yours now. I wish you every luck. I've already transferred your shares to your accounts. If you ever need me, you all know how to find me."

"Enjoy it, Boss."

"What, Max?"

"Retirement."

Carter looked puzzled. He'd not really thought of it like that before, and it brought some sadness to his face. It was clear he was deeply torn between staying and going, but time was creeping up on them all. Mason reached out his hand to the Boss.

"Been an honour."

He shook his hand as Mitchell pulled a cart over to them loaded with the three old timers' gear.

"You sure about this now, Boss?"

"Sure as I ever will be, Mitchell. Good luck, to all of you."

It was time. He grabbed hold of the controls of the cart and walked away with the other two at his side. Mason turned around, looking at the crew who were left.

"You don't feel like joining 'em, Wizard?"

"Hey, I ain't that old yet."

"Fair enough. Glad to hear it."

"What about me?" Erin asked.

"We got you out, and for free I might add. This was your lucky day. The IPA will help you contact your family and get you home."

"I don't have a family to go home to."

"Not my problem."

"So you are just going to leave me here?"

"What more do you want from us? We saved your life and got you here."

"And it'll be worth nothing if you leave me here."

"What are you running from?"

She was silent for a moment, and almost snapped back an answer, but knew she was in danger of revealing more than she wanted to.

"Look, I have nowhere to go. Everything I owned was taken from me when I was kidnapped. Let me go with you, just as far as a VASI colony."

He shook his head, looking at the crew. Mitchell shook his head, but Liu gave him pleading eyes that already made him feel guilty for not trying to help.

"Mitchell, how long till we get across the border to USV territories?"

"Probably a few weeks, depends what work comes up, if any."

"All right, Erin. I know you're hiding things from us. I am not buying this damsel in distress stuff, but we'll give you a ride. Can you cook?"

"Sure."

"Then that's your new job while you're aboard. No idle bodies on this ship, not unless they pay their way."

She scowled at the idea, knowing she could do nothing but accept.

"I can do more, you know."

"I'm sure. You'll have plenty of time to blow our minds with your skills."

They all went silent as she didn't find it funny, and the

others only found it awkward.

"All right, what are we still doing here? Let's move out."

Within an hour, they were sitting at a table in the cargo area with their meal; the same table Skylar had sat at that day. The tone was sombre. The mission had been a complete success, and the pay was good, but the retirement of the three original crewmembers was a dark day for them all.

"This ain't half bad," Mason commented.

Liu chuckled. They both knew it was the best meal they'd had in a good while, and Erin glared at him as a result of knowing it.

"So you're the Captain now?" she asked him.

He looked down at his food and nodded as he took a bite.

"That's the way of it. I've been on this boat longer than anyone, even Wizard. Boss handed the reins over to me, but that don't make it any less a home to the rest. You pull your weight, and you can call it home too, but somehow I doubt you're in this for the long haul."

She shrugged her shoulders and didn't respond.

"So you got a last name?"

"No."

"Your parents not love you enough to pass on the family name?"

"My parents are none of your business," she snapped.

So that struck a nerve!

"All right."

"And you, your given name is Max?"

"Yes. So you said you were in USV territory when you were captured, and that you had everything you owned with you. Explain that to us."

Liu coughed and jabbed his elbow into Mason's side with little subtlety. He turned and answered his friend's reservations.

"No, no. We expect to have a little trust towards those aboard, and I think we deserve to know, after all we have done for this girl."

"Girl? I'm twenty one in a few weeks."

"Okay, well, that's a start. Carry on."

"I was going in search of the last family I have left. My uncle. There was nothing left for me where I was."

"And where was that?"

"Enough for one day. Let the girl rest. Not like we have ever had your life story out," said Liu.

"That's probably because there isn't much to tell."

"With what I saw today, I doubt that," replied Erin.

Three days went by, when the lights began to flicker and power surged through the ship. Mason was asleep at the time and leapt out of bed as it happened. He rushed to the bridge, wearing just his underwear and t-shirt.

"What's going on, Mitchell?"

"We're having power difficulties. This is internal."

He turned to see Wizard stepping aboard the bridge.

His arms and face were filthy from working in the engine bay.

"We gotta problem."

Mason's eyes widened. He could already see he wasn't going to like the news.

"Long story short, we need to put down somewhere with a habitable environment now."

"How long do we have?"

"A minute, an hour, two, it ain't good."

"Christ, how did that happen?" asked Mitchell.

"No goddamn idea. A few things were a little worn no doubt, but nothing would have suggested this."

"Right now, it doesn't matter," Mason said. "Felix, what's the nearest world to here?"

"He tapped his console, searched through, and responded a few seconds later.

"We're in 61 Cigni, so... Krittika..."

"Never heard of it."

"I don't care. If it's got air and a chance of finding components, it'll do."

Liu rushed into the room. "What the hell's going on?"

"Ship's fucked. We have to get to ground ASAP. Gather the suits together. We may need the air."

Liu's face turned to fear. Being stuck in space with no power or air was every traveller's worst fear. Mason knew they all felt as sick in their stomachs as he did.

"How long to reach Krittika?"

"At our current speed about three hours. I don't want to risk using the thrusters anymore. Using the engines for life support is putting enough strain as it is. We need at least a little power to slow our descent."

"We could cut the engines now, use our suits to breathe, and fire them back up when we get there?"

"No, once those engines stop, we aren't likely to get 'em started again without a fair bit of work."

Mason sighed, "So what can we do?"

"Your idea about using the suits isn't a bad one. We could cut all life support systems and reduce the strain on the engines as much as is possible. It might help. Downside is, if the engines do fail en route, we'll already have been using up our oxygen reserves," replied Wizard.

"You remember when I recommended buying that old two-seat fighter a few weeks back. This is exactly the kind of situation we could have done with it," added Felix.

"Yeah, big help."

Erin stepped into the room. She had followed the sounds of the heated discussion and overhead the very end of it.

"How about sending out a distress signal?" she asked.

"From a privately registered small transport in these territories? Anyone who didn't assume we were pirates would be a fool."

"So maybe we pray for a fool?"

"Sorry, princess, we never have that kinda luck. Break

out our suits. Everyone needs to be running on their own air in the next five minutes. Felix, shut everything but the essentials down in two. Wizard, you better be with those engines, and make sure they give us everything they have to give."

Fifteen minutes later, all but Wizard were sitting on the bridge in their space suits. The lighting was down to emergency only. They knew there was nothing to do now but wait. For a long time an uncomfortable silence loomed over the bridge until Erin finally broke it.

"This world we're heading for, what's there?"

"Don't look at me, never heard of the place," replied Mason.

"It's a frontier colony. Back to basics," Felix said. "Says here there was a substantial migration there after Balkatide crystal deposits were discovered in several parts of the world."

"They aren't poor then," replied Liu.

"How so?"

"It's used in construction," said Erin.

"And how would you know something like that?"

"Because I read, Max."

Liu laughed, and Felix couldn't help but join in.

"Laugh it up, junkie."

Felix's smile was instantly removed from his face.

"Hey, that shit ain't funny, man. I thought we just left that crap behind."

"Hope so," he replied. "So go on, what is this Balkatide?"

"A key component in creating the power chips in laser guns, as well as ancillary engine components. and all sorts of other things. With the war, they must be booming," Liu replied.

"Well, we should at least get access to some workshop supplies then. They must have transports in and out all the time."

"Hope so," said Andrews.

"And this world is still in Alliance territory?" Erin asked.

"Afraid so. You seem pretty desperate to get out, why?" asked Mason.

"Because any family or friends I could get help from are that side."

"Yeah, but you aren't a combatant. You could hop on any transport out of here."

She shrugged her shoulders. He could see she was uneasy about the Alliance forces getting hold of her, and that made him suspicious. Liu could see he wanted to pry further so intervened.

"Hey, we all have secrets. She doesn't have to tell us."

"Not unless it puts this crew at risk."

Liu turned to her. "Does it?"

"No," she replied sternly, but Mason wasn't convinced.

The conversation continued and moved on to less stressful and more trivial topics to pass the time, until finally a red blinker light flashed on the console to say they were approaching the world. It was not the hive of activity they had been anticipating. Just one ship could be seen leaving the atmosphere. Had they not known otherwise, they would have doubted the world was inhabited at all.

"One of the first few planets to ever be terraformed," said Felix.

"I suppose you've been doing your reading too?" Mason grinned.

"All the money you got from the last job and others you have done, surely you could buy a new ship?"

"The cost of the operations and the logistics either side are much more than you'd think, Erin," Liu explained.

"And anyway, I like this ship," Mason added.

"You hang on to things so dearly, and they have a habit of breaking your heart," muttered Andrews.

"Hey, she's got us through hell more than a few times. It'll take more than an engine malfunction to end the Foxy Lady's days."

"All ladies get old," he replied.

"Well you're a real cherry bastard today, aren't you?" asked Mason.

"This is it. I'm gonna try and reverse thrust the engines to slow our approach."

"And if it doesn't work?"

"I got another idea, but you're not gonna like it."

"Then make the first plan work."

The engines roared to life as they approached the

atmosphere, but as they got half way through, there were two loud cracks from the engine bays, and the power dropped off.

"Shit this is gonna be rough!"

They burst through the clouds at double the speed they would normally and were heading nose first for a vast salt lake.

"We ain't got a lot of power!"

"Use the landing thrusters."

He hit the switch and it began to reduce their speed, but not quickly enough.

"Deploy the chutes."

"Not at this speed, they'll tear right off."

"Wizard, we need you!"

Mason turned to see Archibald was already gone.

"Six thousand feet!" yelled Felix.

He had got the nose up a little, but there wasn't enough power to get the lift he needed.

"Five thousand!"

"Come on, Wizard," whispered Mason.

"Four Thousand!"

Mason ripped his helmet off and rushed out of the bridge towards the engine bays. Mitchell's voice still echoed through the corridors over the tannoy.

"Three thousand!"

He reached the engine bays. Wizard was drilling through into a compression chamber. He lifted up an electro rod and slipped it into the hole, picked up a huge wrench, and threw it to Mason.

"Two thousand!" came Mitchell's voice.

"Hit that with everything you've got!" yelled Andrews.

"What? How can that work?" yelled Mason.

"Just do it!"

"One thousand metres!"

He got a good grip on the wrench that was a metre and a half long and weighed twenty kilos. Mason swung it back and smashed the rod with every ounce of strength he could muster. Sparks burst from it, and a pulse of electricity rushed down the wrench and into Mason's hands. The shock threw him off his feet and three metres away onto his back where he landed hard. Rolling over to his side, he coughed out a little blood as he heard the engines roar with power.

"Five hundred metres, four, three."

They could feel the engines begin to push the tail down and quickly level them off. Mason looked up at Archibald from the deck and prayed. Twenty seconds went by when they both expected to crash and burn at any second.

"We've done it!"

"Just as the call came over the radio, the engines coughed and spluttered and cut out."

"All right, here we go. Hold on to your asses," said Mitchell.

They hit the ground hard, but a lot lighter than they

had expected. They bounced just a metre off the ground, landing once again with a jolt, and sliding a hundred metres through dirt and dust.

"This is the pilot speaking. Welcome to Krittika. I hope you had a pleasant flight and appreciate the fact you're still alive."

CHAPTER THREE

Mason sat sprawled out on one of the chairs from the hold of the ship. He'd dragged it out into the open air beside their final resting place and also brought the table with him. His right leg was up on the table, and he had a bottle of Beaulieu's reserve in one hand. It was a coarse and unlikeable whiskey liqueur they had gotten a crate of cheap a few months back. It was the only drink available, and he was making the most of the sunshine while drinking it. Wizard strode up to him. He looked even filthier than before, now he'd spent an hour going over the damage.

"Well, how bad is it?"

"Bad. We've got a couple of holes in one of the blocks. The reactor's shot. Inlet manifolds punctured."

Mason's eyes widened.

"Yeah, I'd say we took a few shots back on Sharini when we picked you up. They must have nailed us in the ass. The damage was done and gone unnoticed. It has only got worse."

"Christ, what did they hit us with?"

"Something heavy. Looks like they took one of your trucks, so I guess that would explain it. You should have been long gone before that could have happened."

"That was my fault," replied Erin.

She and Liu were sitting beside the table with Mason.

"Damn right it was," added Mason.

Liu scowled at him.

"Not like she asked to be there," he said.

"Well, nonetheless, it is what it is. Upside is we get to catch a few rays."

"What do we need to get her working?" Liu asked.

"A tonne of components which should cost about fifty k, but God knows what we'll be charged if the dealers know they have us over a barrel. Plus about a week's work."

Mason shook his head.

"All the years of smooth running the Lady has given, us and now we get lumped in the shit."

"They were never that smooth," muttered Andrews.

"Mily okay?"

Erin looked surprised.

"The quadcopter you came in on," Liu clarified.

"One of the Boss' wives?"

"Girlfriend," Mason smiled.

"Yeah, amazingly she didn't take anything but a

few scrapes and burns. She's ready when you are," said Andrews.

"Nearest town is just a few clicks north," stated Mason. "Felix, you know what parts we need?"

"I got a pretty good idea."

"Good, then you're coming with me. We don't know anything about this world, so all of you watch yourselves. Wizard, get working on what you can. Liu, you're on guard duty. We came in pretty hot, so our presence cannot have gone unnoticed."

"You expecting hostility here?"

"I always expect hostility and prepare for everything, Erin."

"It's a little cynical, don't you think?"

"Fact, I'm still alive while many others in this line of work aren't."

She looked to Liu who could not help but agree. Mason turned to leave but was interrupted by Erin.

"Then I can help. I can shoot."

He smirked and laughed a little. "Really? That part of your comprehensive education?"

"Yes," she replied sternly, "I can ride, I can shoot, and I can hunt."

"Anyone ever put you to the test?" he asked, lifting his rifle from the table. He threw it at her with some force. She barely caught it and almost lost her balance.

"This the way you treat all the women you meet?"

Liu laughed, and it was confirmation enough for her. Mason spun around, looking at the landscape. It was a warm climate with a mix of grass, dirt, and dry sand. He spotted a crop of three trees close to a hundred metres away. They were each no more than thirty centimetres wide.

"Put a single shot into each one of those trees, and I'll take you at your word."

"Max..." Liu cut in.

It was a tough challenge, and they all knew it.

"No, no, she said she can hunt. With those kinds of skills, you must be capable of a hundred yard shot. Let's see what she can do," he replied as he turned to her.

"You see we're in the business of fact, not hearsay. If you want our trust, then you must prove you're worth it."

She didn't like his assumption about her character, but it only made her more determined to prove him wrong. She lifted the rifle to her shoulder. The fact she didn't kneel to take the shot made Liu wonder if she was either confident or naive. Her finger squeezed the trigger, and they watched as the laser struck the first tree on the left.

"Lucky shot..." Mason quickly snapped.

Before his words were out, she had put a shot into the other two and left him speechless. She turned around to enjoy her moment. Max did everything he could to recover and hide his amazement.

"Happy?"

"Well, Erin. That might be the first honest thing you've told us since coming aboard. Hang onto the rifle for now."

"Thanks."

"You ever shot a man?"

She shook her head.

"Well I hope you can shoot that well when it counts."

He turned and walked away with Mitchell. Liu stepped up to her, looking highly impressed.

"He likes you."

"Really?"

"Not many people give him reason to be impressed. Well done. You really learned that for hunting?"

"How else?"

"Lot of reasons to learn how to shoot, and most of them aren't for sport."

"I can see why you were a detective."

It was a subtle and clever shift of subject and that amused him. They turned as they heard the rotors fire up, and Mily raced out from the ship with Mitchell at the controls.

"You ever come to places like this much?" she asked.

"We go wherever we can get work. A well off frontier world like this though; it's wealthy enough to manage on its own, not the kind of place I'd expect to see kidnappings."

"That all the work you do?"

He shook his head. "If it needs some muscle, and they pay enough, it's work for us."

"And what about right or wrong?"

"Its a grey area. We would turn a job town if it were against our principles."

"Turned down any work recently?"

He shook his head.

* * *

It was just a thirty-minute ride to the town, and as they approached, they could see it was a small place.

"Really think we'll find what we need here?" asked Mason.

"Pretty sure. They have to keep ships moving on mineral rich worlds like this. We'll make it work."

The town was mostly constructed of metal prefabricated complexes that looked like they'd been there for many decades. There was no guarded entrance or security of any kind, let alone a perimeter wall. It looked big enough for a population of up to a thousand.

"Can't get a lot of crime around here," Mitchell commented.

"I'll believe that when I see it. Just remember, some of these worlds aren't too friendly to newcomers."

"Perhaps we should have brought rifles?"

"No, be ready for a fight, but don't go looking. If we need more than our sidearms, then things really are bad."

Quadcopters and wheeled trucks alike were rolling

in and out of town at a steady rate. It was clear it was a mining town and running steadily. A few turned to look as they entered the main high street of the small town. The main streets had been concreted in a stark contrast to the dusty roads outside the populated area. Mason noted how the people he saw all appeared comfortably off, if not dripping in wealth.

"We aren't gonna get anything cheap here," whispered Mitchell.

"Nope, but I'll be happy to get in the air at any cost."

"I'd hold that thought until you've heard the prices."

A line of vehicles was parked outside what appeared to be a bar.

"Pull up there."

"Sure?"

"Yeah, we need information, and in a little place like this, the local watering hole is the place to go."

"If you say so, Boss."

They looked at each other in surprise. It was the first time he'd ever been called it by the crew. Mitchell didn't know whether to apologize or not. They both thought about it for a moment.

"I may be Captain of the Foxy Lady now, but there was only ever one Boss. This is our first time of going at it alone, so let's do it right."

The name of the establishment was the Digger, a rather uninspired choice, considering the location. It was a three storey complex with a hand held mining drill hanging from the name post as its mascot. Inside, they found tall ceilings, and it had been decorating lovingly with artefacts from several worlds. There was enough seating for a hundred, but only eight people were sitting or standing around the bar. Mason noted a young woman several tables away from the rest, harbouring her glass. She looked brooding and serious, but was of slight figure and seemed of little threat, despite her angry eyes.

They passed the woman and reached the bar. The barman looked afraid the second he spotted them. He looked down at the guns slung on their sides and at their dusty clothing.

"What can I do for you boys?" he asked.

"Couple of beers and info on who could supply us with some ship components."

The colour seemed to return to his face, and he suddenly mellowed and reached for a glass.

"Sorry, I thought you were here for something else."

The man's fear made him curious, but he knew not to pry when they had just arrived and had no business there.

"You come with that ship that came down hard to the south of here a little earlier?"

Mason nodded.

"Can't have been your intention to come here. Not many folks do who aren't here for business. What line of work you in?"

"Transport."

His eyebrow rose. "A ship that small, and yet you wear that gun like you were born with it."

Mason smiled.

He's quick and smart.

"We specialise in high risk valuable goods. Some folk around would try and rob us in our work."

"Mmm, ain't that the truth?" one of the patrons snorted.

"Really? Mason asked. "Looks like a pretty safe town to me."

"It ain't outsiders we gotta worry about."

Mason knew it was the time to stop asking. He could feel trouble brewing that they did not need.

"Sorry to hear about that, friend."

The man nodded wearily and took a slug of his drink.

"I'm Porter Kaperon, and I own this place. Have done since it opened. Most folk round here call me Kaper."

The bar owner was in his late fifties, tall, and with a solid round stomach. He had not a hair left on his head. His cheeks were red, and he was seemingly a cheery man but with some big worries in the world. He carefully placed two tankards of beer before them. It was a surprise, for they rarely ever saw anything but acrylic beakers. Too few drinking establishments trusted their patrons with breakable containers.

"Twenty credits."

It wasn't cheap, but then the drinks looked so appetizing it was making his mouth water. He quickly handed over the change and lifted the glass to take a sip. Mitchell was surprised to see hard currency, but he didn't question it.

"Oh!"

It was well chilled and smooth, and only reminded him quite how cheap and nasty the Beaulieu's reserve was.

"Guy could get used to life in a place like this," said Mitchell.

"Mmm," the barkeep muttered hesitantly. "So you need parts? Couple of places in town, but only one has anything for a Leander."

Mason was surprised to hear he knew the classification of their ship.

"I've done more than my share of space travel you know," he added. "Alpha Factors is where you want to go. Head to the east side of town, and keep going for half a kilometre. It's a big old warehouse. Guy who runs is it is called Avery Ryant. He'll sort you out."

"Well, thanks for that, "Mason said and lifted his glass from the bar.

"You feel like a refill, let me know."

The two of them turned from the bar and sat down at a nearby table, facing each other. From Mason's seat he was looking right at the mysterious woman they'd past on the way in. She was slim and athletic. A long coat covered much of her skin, but he could see tattoos on the back of her hand that vanished beneath her sleeve and were visible on her neck. She looked young, but far from clueless. Her skin was pale and hair jet black. She didn't fit on the mining world at all, which made him all the more curious. She had the look of someone who had experienced the galaxy, but appeared so young to have done so.

She suddenly turned and looked into his eyes. Her gaze was that of daggers. It was a deadly look that seemed backed up by whatever confidence and experience lay behind her eyes. Mitchell turned to see what had gotten Mason so locked in intrigue.

He smiled. "Looks like she wants to kill you."

"Wouldn't be the first," he replied softly.

Their interest was broken as heavy footsteps passed through the open doors. The room fell silent, and Mason and Mitchell looked at the three men who had stepped inside. They were covered in dust and had clearly been on the road. Mason looked around and saw Kaper recognised them instantly. He had the same fearful look as when they had arrived, but this time he knew these men.

"Afternoon!" one yelled, as they paced up to the bar.

He strutted forward, and Mason could tell by the man's greasy-looking expression that he was not a likeable character. He stopped at the woman's table and stood over her, waiting and expecting her to look up. When he didn't get a response, he slammed his fist onto the table. She didn't even flinch, and that further fuelled Mason's curiosity towards her. Finally, she looked up with a glare, picked up her drink, and sipped it. She stared him down without a word until he finally realised he wasn't getting anywhere.

"Three beers!" he shouted.

Kaper fumbled with glasses. He appeared to be uncomfortable with their presence, fearing the newcomers. They turned to Mason and Mitchell who were both looking right back at them.

"Some new faces in town today. Always good to see money coming into the area!"

Mason nodded back in agreement. His hand wanted to reach for the grip of his pistol in readiness, as he could already feel there was something bad afoot. The three men acted as if they owned the establishment, or at least had some major power over its owner. They continued on to the bar to get the drinks. Mason was suddenly aware of how quiet the bar had gotten. Nobody spoke a word.

"Merry bunch," whispered Mitchell.

The leader of the group had heard the mutterings but not understood what had been said. He turned with an inquisitive stare.

"So, what brings you boys to town?"

"Got a few engines problems. Looking for parts to get us on our way," Mason answered.

"And her? She with you?"

Mason shrugged his shoulders, shaking his head as he

looked over to the lone woman.

"A girl should never drink alone."

She didn't respond, and the man was growing tired of trying to get a response. He turned back to Kaper who was awaiting his every request.

"Well hand it over."

Kaper knelt down behind the bar and came back up with a small rigid carry case.

"Here it is, Mr Herschel, Sir."

He opened the box, and despite Mason not being able to see the contents from his seat, it was evident to them all that it was money. Kaper was being squeezed by whoever Herschel was, and it left a bad taste in the back of his mouth. Mitchell leaned in close.

"Credit chips?"

"Still popular on these worlds where e-transactions can't be guaranteed. Hard currency goes a long way. Plus it's untraceable."

"This isn't right. They're being robbed."

"It's not our fight, not our business."

Mason could see trouble brewing, and he knew they had no way to leave the planet once it began. He tried with all his will to ignore his instinct to give Herschel what was coming to him.

"Yeah," Herschel grunted triumphantly.

He turned around to look at Mason once again, having heard the two muttering.

"So that ship that came down this morning must be yours. I do hope you get her fixed up. Stay more than three days and we start charging."

"For what?" Mason asked quickly.

The man's face tightened, and his tone became angry.

"For the privilege of parking your arse on the land of Mr Volkov."

"And he owns this world, does he?"

"The other two chuckled under their breath."

"Yes he does, actually," replied Herschel.

Mason leant back, resting his foot on the table before them, in a deliberate move to show he was not intimidated.

"You see, in my line of work, payment is made for a service. You provide us a service, and we'll pay the appropriate cost."

"I'm starting to think we've got a hero here," Herschel said to his friends. They laughed in response.

"Mr Volkov doesn't appreciate heroes. They have a tendency to get shot in the back."

"So he's a man of principle, as well?" asked Mason sarcastically.

Out of the corner of his eye, he could see the mysterious woman grin a little. It was the most emotion he had seen from her since they arrived. It angered Herschel further, but he could see Mason was of stronger stuff than the townsfolk. He turned back to Kaper.

"This the kind of customer you cater for these days.

Rude, disrespectful, and loud mouthed. Well that's gonna cost you. Rent just doubled for this month."

"That's some cold shit," Mitchell stated.

Herschel spun around quickly.

"The black one speaks. You feel so bad for him you can always pay the bill! Well, what'll it be?"

Mitchell looked to Mason, who shook his head.

"Father, I'm going out for a..."

They all turned to see a well-dressed woman, who couldn't have been much more than sixteen years old, step out from a room behind the bar. She stopped when she realised she'd walked in on a situation she'd rather not have seen.

"Ah, the barkeep's daughter. Kimby, isn't it? You have flowered," Herschel sneered. "What was that last week, your seventeenth birthday?"

Mason could see sweat dripping down Kaper's face. He was gone from uncomfortable and scared to truly fearful.

"Answer Mr Herschel," he said, his voice shaking.

"Yes, Sir," she replied, lowering her eyes. She appeared to be a well brought up and educated girl.

"Mr Volkov has been asking about you of late. Would you like a personal visit?"

She looked at her father for an answer, and Mason could tell he was terrified of saying no.

"Well?"

Finally, Kaper looked up with a little defiance in his

eyes.

"No. You've had more than enough from us today. You can't have my daughter as well."

"No!" he yelled.

"He stepped up to the bar and reached in to grab Kaper by the collar of his shirt. He hauled the man off his feet and over the bar. Kaper landed hard on his back a few metres from where Mason sat.

"Who are you to deny the will of Colonel Michael Volkov?" he screamed.

"Please, you can't!" he cried.

Herschel lifted his boot and slammed it down on Kaper's face. The impact burst his nose and smashed the back of his head against the floor. He cowered into a ball, holding his bloody nose and began to cry.

"Father!" Kimby screamed and rushed to his side.

Herschel turned and slapped her across the face. It wasn't a hard hit, but enough to make her recoil and wince in pain. It was also enough for Mason, and all he could take. He kicked the chair before him forward, causing it to slide into Herschel. The back hit him in the stomach and made him buckle slightly.

"How about you pick on someone your own size!"

Mason was on his feet like lightening and bearing down on the unscrupulous thug. He grabbed Herschel at his shoulders, drove a knee hard into his chest, and then hit him with an uppercut to the chin. It sent him crashing back against the bar where he had so recently dragged Kaper from.

The other two thugs were in utter shock and took a moment to respond. One reached for his pistol but fumbled. He'd clearly never had to draw on someone in his life. They were men practiced in the arts of intimidation and nothing more. Mitchell launched his glass at the man hitting his shoulder. The glass smashed and splintered over the thug, giving him enough time to rush forward and deliver a quick hook into his nose.

Mason quickly drew his pistol on the other man and shot the pistol he was drawing from his belt. It split in half, and the thug dropped it from the pain of the heat of the blast. Mason quickly spun the pistol around in his grip, so that he held it by the barrel, and smashed the grip across his opponent's face. The impact was enough to knock him unconscious.

He turned to see Mitchell was wrestling the other goon. The pilot had never been much of a fighter. He holstered his pistol and grabbed the nearest chair, crashing it down on the man with all his might. The metal chair buckled on impact and smashed the man down to the ground.

They turned back just in time to see Herschel coming at them and wielding a knife. Seemingly out of nowhere, the mysterious young woman appeared and got a grasp of the weapon and spun under Herschel's arm, forcing his shoulder up. He screamed in pain as his shoulder clicked out of joint. The woman spun back around and as she did, grabbed hold of the nearest glass tankard. She smashed it over his head, knocking him out cold. The despicable man tumbled to the ground like a sack of bricks. He landed hard beside Kaper who was still cupping his bleeding nose.

Mason looked down at the young woman in surprise. He had known she was far from normal when they first arrived, but it had still surprised him. She was five foot six, and of slim build, yet she had just taken a thickset thug down with ease.

She's a trained professional, no doubt, but in what? Mason asked himself.

"Thanks," he said to her.

"No problem," she replied calmly and went back to her table to finish her drink.

Mason reached down and helped Kaper to his feet. The barkeep looked around in astonishment at the carnage around him.

"What have you done?" he asked fearfully.

"Nothing more than they deserved," replied Mason.

"Do you know what Volkov will do to us for this? You should leave now. I'll tell them you were passing through. We have no idea who you are anyway."

"You can't let anyone shove you around like that, and anyway, we aren't going anywhere. Ship's broken, remember?"

Kaper shook his head.

"He'll kill you for this. He might even kill us for being a part of it."

Mason shook his head in disbelief. He didn't want to get involved, but he seemingly had no choice anymore.

"Who is this Volkov?"

Colonel Volkov. He's the sheriff of the mining towns of this world.

"A military man in a policing role?"

"He is neither. He awarded his rank himself and wasn't elected to his position either. He was one of the first merchants to get working here and has now taken charge of everything."

"So you just keep paying him whatever he asks?"

"All the businesses do. I run a twenty-man mining operation. Volkov takes a fifty percent share in all profits."

"Must be a fortune with the resources here."

"Yes. We are not a poor town, only half as rich as we should be."

"And nobody will do anything about it?"

"Who?" Volkov has hundreds of soldiers at his disposal. He even has the support of the local Alliance forces. We have tried to hire mercenaries to help us, but nobody will do it, not at any price."

Kaper reached over the bar, grabbed a bottle of spirits and some tumblers, and joined them at their table. He poured out the first glass and knocked it back before handing the bottle to Mason.

"How often do they rob you?" he asked.

"End of every month, just after the transports make their pickup and make payment."

"Assholes," added Mitchell.

"You've kicked the hornets' nest here. I suggest you get the parts you need and leave while you still can."

"I was just thinking the same."

"What about those three?" asked Mitchell.

They were beginning to stir. Herschel was the first up. He got to his knees and immediately recognised Mason, remembering what had happened. His hand reached down his pistol, but he found an empty holster. He looked over and could see the line of pistols on the table where Mason was sitting.

"You know what you've done? You've fucked with the wrong people," he snarled.

Mason shook his head.

"You just don't know when to quit, do you? You're going to go back to this Volkov, and tell him to stop robbing the people of this town. Or, I'll make sure my friends in the IPA hear about this, you hear?"

"Go to hell, you..."

Mason drew his pistol quickly from his holster while still sitting and fired before Herschel could finish his sentence. The laser hit him square in the chest and killed him instantly. Mason was on his feet as the body was hitting the ground. Kaper was too stunned to speak. Max stepped up to the other two that were with Herschel.

"You'll tell your boss to leave these people alone and pass on the message?"

They nodded quickly.

"Now get the hell out of here!"

They staggered to their feet and rushed out of the bar, looking back in shock at Herschel's body sprawled out across the floor.

"What have you done?" pleaded Kaper.

"The damage was already done. Now they've got something real to worry about. With any luck, they'll think twice about extorting you further. Worst case, they'll think we were a couple of crazy travellers who have come and gone, and nothing changes."

He stood up and knocked back his drink. He wasn't sure what kind of spirit it was, but it tasted good.

"Let's go," he said to Mitchell.

Kaper and his daughter were still in shock, and the other patrons sat with their mouths wide open at the violent scene that had unfolded before them.

"Wait!" called Kaper.

They stopped. He grabbed a box of beer from beside the bar and handed it to Mason.

"We pay our debts."

He nodded in thanks and then carried on. As they reached the tattooed woman's table, she looked up and finally addressed them.

"I like your style."

"You look like you can handle yourself pretty good. We're down a few crew, and it doesn't look like this is your kinda place. Want a job?" Mason asked.

"Best offer I've heard all day."

She got up and followed them out.

"Name's Mason. This is Mitchell."

"Hella Torres, you can call me Hell."

"Wow, you really are a cheery one," replied Mason.

CHAPTER FOUR

'Alpha Factors'. The shop was just where Kaper said it would be. It was a large warehouse. The lower three metres of the perimeter of the structure couldn't be seen for the mounds of ship parts stacked in the open air around it.

"You remember what we need?" asked Mason.

Felix lifted up his datapad with the list he had made. Hella leaned in to see it for herself.

"That's quite a list."

"We got into a little trouble on our last job. It can be dangerous work what we do."

"Yeah, and what sort of work is that?"

"Don't worry, you'll love it."

Mitchell smiled at Mason's vague response. Hella seemed curious enough to go along with it, and they both got a sense she had little holding her to anything in the universe, not work, family, or money.

They stepped inside and found a man of Kaper's age. He was lying back in a chair and watching the news. A space battle was being reported far from where they were.

"That the kind of work you're in?" Hella asked.

"Sort of, but we get paid better, and owe allegiance to nobody but ourselves."

"Sounds perfect."

Mason nodded in agreement, as the man heard their voices and turned to greet them. He was wiry, with deep blue eyes and wore an old dirty and faded boiler suit.

"Welcome! I'm Avery Ryant."

"Kaper from the Digger sent us."

"Ah, yes, what can I do for you?"

Mason gestured for Mitchell to continue.

"We've got a Leander class transport in a bit of a bad way, hoping you can provide us with some parts."

"Leander? Oh, yeah, I have parts for 'em. Don't get a lot of call for them anymore, though. Most of the freighters coming in and out of here are a good bit larger. You aren't in the mining business, are you?"

"No, Sir."

"Well, let's see what you need."

He passed the datapad over.

"Shit," Ryant replied in a long drawn out manner, "that's a long list. How'd you even reach this world if you needed all this?"

"Barely," replied Mitchell.

"You're lucky you didn't die up there. Your maintenance not being kept up or something?"

"Nope, we got a good mechanic, but we're in a dangerous business. Some unscrupulous bastards put a few heavy laser shots into our ass not so long ago."

"You're not in some kind of trouble with the authorities are you?"

"Uhhh..."

"Cos it would be okay if you were. Authorities of this world are low life thieving scum. Hell, you come to blows with them, and I'd give you a discount."

Mitchell opened his mouth to spill the beans, but Mason shook his head to stop him.

"Mr Ryant, we're in a bit of a rush to patch up our vessel and get on about our business."

"Yes," he replied dubiously. "I got most of the parts you want here, and you can take 'em now. But the coil you're after, I'll have to source that elsewhere."

"All right, get us a price, and we'll do business."

Ryant turned to his console and tapped in a number of keys as he yelled into the warehouse.

"Cayne! Get your ass up here!"

He finally turned back to Mason.

"Including the coil, which I'm pretty sure I can get for a good price, that'll be forty eight thousand."

Hella took a deep breath, and Mason could see she was expecting the need to find an alternative lift off the world.

"That's fine," he replied, lifted his datapad, and pulled his credit card from the side.

"This going to go through?" Ryant asked, doubtfully. "Not a whole lot of trust round here, is there?"

"Well, okay."

He fed the card into his console and put the transaction through. His eyes widened when the information displayed on the screen confirmed Mason was a reliable client.

"Gone through fine. Cayne will be up with your stuff in just a few moments. I'll head out now to negotiate for that coil. You want it delivered?"

"That'd be good. We're a few kilometres south of town. You can get my comms number from the card."

"I'll get on it immediately. Good doing business with you."

The components filled out the quadcopter and barely left space for Hella to squeeze into one of the seats.

"Shit load of money for a few pieces of junk metal," she stated.

"Actually, that was a fair price. Surprisingly fair," replied Mitchell.

"And you, Mason. You didn't have to get involved in their troubles back there. Why did you?"

"Maybe because I could see good folks being hustled, and that doesn't sit right with me."

"But you're a gun for hire, aren't you?"

He looked back at her, surprised. "You're a sharp one,

aren't you?"

"So why did you help them for free?"

"Well they did pay us in good liquor," he replied, smiling.

"You're not like any mercenary I have ever known."

"And you have known many, have you?"

"Enough."

Her vagueness continued to irritate him, but also fuelled his interest in her. The sun was going down by the time they reached the ship. Liu, Erin and Andrews were sitting at the table Mason had pulled out earlier that day, and they had started a fire beside them. Mitchell pulled up close by and leapt off to find they were enjoying a cup of something warm. He dragged out the crate of beer and dumped it on the table between them.

"Here, we've got some good stuff."

Their attention was quickly drawn to the newcomer. Hella was like a shadow in the dim light, with her black hair and dark coat.

"This is Hella. Looks like she'll be joining us."

Liu looked up. She was nothing like anything he'd expect to see in a colleague.

"Ben Liu," he said as a welcome. Though he wasn't at all convinced Mason hadn't just brought her along because she was a pretty face.

Mason continued to introduce them and then got to Erin.

"Another new face among us. Erin is hitching a lift."

Hella looked down at the rifle that was still resting across her lap.

"Know how to use that?"

The others laughed.

"Went through that earlier today, and she sure can," Liu grinned.

"Well, this crew just keeps getting younger," Andrews said.

It was true. Mason had been one of the youngest aboard for so many years, and now he was a seasoned veteran among them.

"A bit of new blood can't hurt," he added.

Mitchell ripped open the box and found glass bottles inside. He handed them out one by one.

"Wow, posh stuff," said Liu. "How much this set you back?"

"Nothing at all. It was gift," replied Mason.

Liu looked at him with a suspicious expression.

"And what did you do to receive such a gift?"

"Just helped out where we could."

"Mmm," Liu muttered. "Do I really want to know?"

"Probably not."

They each prised the caps off and clashed the bottles together before slugging them back and appreciating the fine taste. The fire was a nice touch that they all appreciated. It wasn't a cold night, but it was a comfort they rarely got to enjoy.

"So, Hella, where you from?" asked Liu.

"Lots of places."

"Family?"

"Dead."

It lowered the tone to a sombre one that Mason tried to move past.

"You handled yourself like a trained fighter back there. Where did you learn those skills?"

"Fighting? What did you get yourself into?" asked Liu.

"Hey, we just went to a bar for info. We didn't start anything."

"An unknown world and you go to a bar to find info?" asked Andrews. "When will you ever learn? How many times have you got out of a bar without a fight?"

"Yeah, but this was daytime. I didn't expect to find cause for trouble."

"And yet you found it anyway," added Liu.

"What can I say? I seem to attract bad sorts."

Hella nodded in agreement which made Erin laugh.

"You may act like a tough guy, but you have a soft heart Mason," she stated.

Mason looked around in surprise at the crew.

"Back to you," Liu said to Hella. "What are these skills he's talking about?"

"I trained on Melian III."

Liu sat up quickly. "Melian III?"

"What of it?" asked Mason.

"Melian is a world for training assassins, spies, espionage skills. Intelligence operatives. What on earth would you be doing there?"

"Do you tell everyone you meet your life's story?" she asked.

They all went silent. Liu was suspicious of her story, but Mason realised there may be some truth to it after what he'd seen her do.

"So another secretive one aboard. You and Erin should get along just great."

Hella looked over to Erin. The two were eyeing each other up and seemed to have little in common. They looked to be from completely different cultures and walks of life. Hella shrugged her shoulders.

"Whoever said you had to like someone to work with them?"

Liu chuckled, "Amen. I wouldn't be here otherwise. Mason can be a son of a bitch."

"You're a cop?" asked Hella of Liu.

He squinted. "Why would you say that?"

"You are, aren't you?"

"Used to be, how could you tell?"

"Besides the obvious, there's a warrant up for your arrest in VASI territories. Twenty thousand credits being offered for your capture."

He suddenly sat upright and looked over to Mason.

"What the hell are you here for? To collect my head?"

he snapped and stood up, kicking his chair back.

"Whoa!" yelled Mason, stepping in between them. He looked around, but Hella still sat in a relaxed manner.

"Well? That why you're here?"

"Wouldn't have said so if I was."

"Yes or no?"

"No."

He turned back to Liu.

"That good enough for you?"

He shrugged, picked up his chair, and sat back down.

"So, a cop wanted by the cops. You are an interesting one," she smiled.

"Hey, there aren't any saints among us."

"Good, because I don't play by anyone's rules, Mason."

Mason knocked back his beer, grabbed another and spoke to Andrews.

"Where are you up to with the work?"

"I've made a solid start. I'll need all of tomorrow to remove the rest of the fried parts, and then we can make a start on the rebuild. You got everything we need?"

"Except for the coil, and that is being delivered to us."

"You paid for that?"

"Yeah."

"And you trust whoever it was to deliver?"

"Got to have some trust in this world," replied Mason. "Otherwise what are we?"

"Cautious," he replied.

"So, you said about a job?" Hella asked.

"Yeah, five percent take on all jobs while you are aboard and actively working. Plus a room and good company."

"And if that doesn't work for me?"

"Then you are welcome to leave anytime. We take on missions of a dangerous nature. I expect you to follow my orders and be there for the rest of the crew. Do that, and we'll get along just fine."

"Sounds like one big happy family."

"Pretty much. Come on, I'll show you to your room."

He got up and led her back towards the ship. They got to the ramp and found it was still running on auxiliary power, and that meant for low lighting.

"I can't speak much for Erin because she's only just come aboard, but the rest are a good tight crew. You can trust them with your lives, and they will expect the same of you while you take a share of the profit."

She nodded in agreement. They reached one of the doors at the side of the cargo bay. It had nothing more than a large number six inscribed on it. He turned the wheel and slid it open.

"This room will be yours for as long as you continue to serve on the ship."

"And what is it you want me to do as part of this crew?"

"The work we do is pretty varied, but as I said, you can generally expect it to be dangerous. It can range from transport of valuable goods to protection details, rescue missions, and all sorts."

"And you think I am up to that?"

"Aren't you?"

"You tell me, Captain," she replied, throwing off her coat.

She wore a close fitting tank top beneath, and he could now see the extent of her tattoos. He didn't recognise any of them, and several looked like nothing more than artistic swirls to him, but he suspected they held more meaning than he realised. Two knives were attached either side of the buckle of her trousers. They were well concealed so that only someone like him would notice them. Yet there was not a gun in sight. He pulled out his sidearm.

"You know how to use one of these?"

"Yeah, but it's not my preferred weapon of choice."

"Ever killed anyone?"

"Yes."

"With a gun?"

"No."

That's surprising. She seems far too young to be the trained killer she appears to be, and yet nothing's giving me any reason to doubt it.

"You're part of this crew now, and I expect you to be capable with a range of common weapons. I already have a pilot, and I have a mechanic. Everyone else is the muscle."

"And Erin, what is she, your girlfriend?"

"She is....she. Actually, I don't know what she is. She's a girl catching a lift till we get to VASI territory."

"You always pick up girls in bars and put them to work?"

He smiled. "I wish. So we good?"

She looked around the room and seemed not accustomed to having her own space.

"So what's next?"

"We get the ship patched up and then look for work."

"Got anything lined up?"

"I got a few ideas."

He walked out of the room but could not help but think about the mysterious nature surrounding the newest crewmember. He got back out to the cargo bay. Liu was waiting for him. He could see the questioning eyes of the former detective.

"Think it's a good idea bringing her in?"

"Not like anyone of us is perfect, Ben. We've all got a past that is far from being that. She is capable and willing to work. We're down a few good men right now."

"I hope you're right," he said and made to go past.

Mason put out his hand and stopped him.

"Hey, when am I ever wrong?" he asked with a smile.

Liu groaned in disapproval as he continued on. Mason was tired, and it had felt like a hell of a long day. Despite this, he could now rest knowing that everything was in motion to get the Foxy Lady patched up and in the air before long. He walked over to his room and put his hand on the door, forgetting he'd moved. He had taken the

Boss' old room that was marked up as number one. He'd lived in the same room for so many years it felt strange to take his mentor's place.

Room one was only thirty percent bigger than the rest, but it certainly made a difference. It had taken just fifteen minutes to move in, for like the rest of the crew, he had few possessions. He rarely had the need to purchase anything that wasn't for his work. He thought of the Boss finally retiring to another life. He too had amassed a good amount of money over the years, but nothing like Carter.

What will I do when the time comes to give it all up? The very idea of leaving everything I know behind is more than a little disconcerting. I just hope the Boss has gone on to better things.

* * *

The morning came quickly. Mason had slept well after the tiring day. He awoke to the smell of fresh air and coffee; a refreshing start he was unaccustomed to. He pulled on his shirt and gun belt and stepped out to find a fresh pot of coffee and several mugs on a table at the centre of the room. Most of the crew were sitting around it.

"Well, I'll be damned, and who do we have to thank for this?"

"Liu pointed to Erin."

"You gave me a job to do while I'm aboard, and I'm doing it," she stated.

She poured a mug full and passed it to him as he walked over to join them. He took a deep sniff of the aroma arising from the hot drink.

"Ahh," he said and turned to the exit ramp, looking at the daylight creeping in.

"Lot to be said for living in a place like this."

"You mean where the people get extorted by the local authorities?" Mitchell asked.

"Well, not that part."

He looked around and could see all the familiar faces were there, bar Andrews who he knew would already be at work on the engines.

"Who's on watch?"

"Hell."

"Who?"

"You know, the brooding young girl you employed yesterday."

"Ah, yeah. Okay, then."

"Someone is approaching from the north."

He spun around to see Hella on the ramp. He'd not even heard her approach and nearly spilt his coffee in surprise. He thought to mention the fact but didn't want to play to her ego. He acted cool and calm as if he'd known she was there.

"How many?"

"One truck with two occupants. Ryant's logo on the side."

"All right, that should be our coil."

He turned back to the others.

"This should be the last component which stands between us leaving this rock."

He quickly paced down the ramp to greet the approaching vehicle. It was indeed Avery and his assistant Cayne. He was surprised to see the boss of the operation along for the ride. They pulled up just a few metres from the ramp of the ship.

"Good morning, Captain!" Avery called out.

He was unusually merry and cheerful which made Mason suspicious.

"Cayne, get the coil unloaded for the Captain!"

His assistant rushed to go about his work. Ryant beckoned for Mason to join him for a personal conversation. He obliged and walked over and away from the truck.

"The parts working okay for you, Captain?"

He was wary of the excessively friendly tone of the man's voice and could tell he was fishing for something.

"You didn't need to come here, Ryant. The coil is paid for. So what do you want?"

"Kaper told me about what you did at his place."

"Yeah, so what?"

"So what? You stood up to the bastards around here that nobody else would."

Mason moved closer quickly to talk more quietly.

"Hey, I didn't champion your cause. I gave some scumbags their due. We're getting out of here as soon as we're fixed up. I don't want anything to do with the shit you're in."

"You obviously care, or you wouldn't have stepped in to help Kaper and his daughter."

Mason sighed. He knew he was digging himself into a deep hole.

"The town traders have assembled and asked me to get you along for a chat. All I ask is you come with me and hear them out."

He turned away and looked back to the ship. He could see Liu and Erin watching him while the others helped unload the coil. He didn't want to land them in the sort of trouble he knew they were on the cusp of facing.

"I think you know the kind of troubles we face in this town. I doubt it's the first time you have seen them. What would you have us do?"

"Arm yourselves and fight back, or pack up and leave."

"And if fighting back meant us dying? You may be experienced fighters, but none of us are. We're merchants."

"We aren't good Samaritans. We're merchants too. We're in business to make money, not give charity."

"And I wasn't asking for it. This town has a lot of money to give. We could be more than reasonable in compensating you for your efforts. Please come with me to town and just hear us out."

"How reasonable are we talking?"

"I'm guessing you're a crew paid to work jobs where guns are a way of life. How much were you paid for your last job?"

"A million credits."

"We could offer you that as a down payment."

His eyes widened in shock, and his concerns for letting his more charitable side overcome him were set aside.

"I'm listening. I'll come in to town, but I'll follow you in my own ride."

"Well, okay, thank you. I really mean it. You don't know the kind misery we've been put through the last few years."

"I'm not promising anything. I'll meet with your people, and we'll take it from there."

"Thank you, really."

He walked past Avery towards the crew who were waiting to hear what he had gotten them into.

"What does he want?"

"Looks like he has a job for us."

"And?"

"I'm gonna follow him into town, Liu, and see what the deal is."

"Alone?"

"Well, you need to help Wizard with the repairs. Hella can handle guard duty for now. She's shown she is capable."

"I'll go with you," said Erin.

Mason looked at her and tried to make sense of her

sudden interest. She seemed eager to get involved since they had recruited Hella.

"What the hell, a pretty face can't do any harm. You're on."

Liu didn't look at all impressed.

"Can I speak with you for a moment?" he asked.

"Yeah, sure."

They paced over the dry ground so they stood a good ten metres away from the ship. Liu looked back and could see Hella looking on. He gestured for Mason to continue on a little further. Hella seemed to have an uncanny ability to hear everything that went on and they knew it. They continued on another ten metres before finally stopping to continue their conservation.

"So what's up?"

"You really have to ask?"

"Come on, cough it up. I can't take the silent treatment."

"I haven't been to town, but you have. Everything you say would suggest this town is being muscled by some major player, resources, soldiers, weapons, and power. You are thinking of taking a job where we'll be outnumbered by what, twenty to one?"

"I don't know."

"That's the point. You don't know. Carter vetted the jobs carefully, as you know. We took what was sensible. We took jobs we could handle. We're down a few crew and looking at a dangerous situation."

"I don't know quite what we are facing here. Only thing I do know is that these people are being walked over, and they're offering a tonne of cash to give them a hand."

"No research, no intel, and most importantly, influenced by the client. You feel for them."

"Don't you? Don't tell me as a former cop, you don't feel like helping these people?"

"Sure, I feel like calling in some help and getting this sorted. But we aren't the guys to do it."

Mason shook his head. "How far have you fallen?"

"What?"

"You took a vow to help those in need and uphold the law, have you forgotten?"

"My employers did."

"And that matters?"

"What do you care? We do jobs for money. We don't uphold the law. We don't follow moral code. We don't serve the people!"

"Really? And you think working as a cop is so much different. You might have liked the feel of 'doing good', but in the end it was just a job!"

"And so what, you're such the fucking good guy now?"

Liu looked away and ran his hands through his hair as he tried to cool off. Finally, he turned around, but Mason interrupted before he could speak.

"You told me that as a cop your hands were tied from helping those you felt needed it. Now we have the chance to help, and nobody is tying our hands, and we stand to make a lot of money from it. You risked your life all the time for crappy pay. Now you have a chance to be on the right side of your moral standpoint, and make a tonne of money at the same time. What's not to like?"

Liu took a deep breath and calmed himself.

"I'm not against helping those who need it. But look around. The crew has survived this far because we took the smart jobs at the right price. We can't save everyone. I learned that."

"Then let me go and suss this one out. I'll see what they want, what we face, and what they're willing to pay. Then I'll bring it to the table, and we'll make a decision as a crew."

"You do that, and definitely take Erin with you. She doesn't seem to have such a bad influence on you."

"And what's that supposed to mean?"

"All I'm saying is that if you accept this call for help, you put her life on the line, same as the rest of us."

"And you think I would do that if it wasn't an acceptable risk?"

Liu smirked. "You know what I learned on the force. An acceptable risk is one that puts others in danger to meet your own goals. But that isn't us, and isn't you. If you commit to something, you put your own ass on the line, same as the rest of us. Remember that. I didn't sign up to throw my life away for no good reason."

Mason nodded in agreement.

"I get you. Hold down the fort. We won't be long."

"I hope so."

Mason started to to walk away but stopped after a few paces.

"You know, when you first joined us, you wanted nothing more than to help those in need. Josiah almost died, after we went back for a kid and his mother that you insisted couldn't be left behind. What happened?"

"Maybe I realised there will always be evil, and I can't stop it all. We're in this for ourselves. We can't save the whole world."

'Maybe you'll have a chance yet."

Mason took a deep breath and thought about it for a moment.

"I can't say we're a beacon of humanity and the pinnacle of moral conduct. But maybe, just maybe you'll have a time to proof yourself yet. You told me you were fired for trying to do the right thing, you remember?"

"Yeah," he replied hesitantly.

"So you were a good cop in a bad world?"

"Yeah."

"Then a chance for redemption is perhaps not impossible."

"You talk pretty righteously for a man who works solely for money."

Mason walked away, smiling.

"Erin!" he shouted.

She jumped to attention with Mason's rifle held across both arms.

"You're with me. We're heading into town."

She jumped to his side and followed him to the quadcopter. Cayne fired up the engine of Ryant's truck.

"I thought we were setting off this world as soon as we could?"

"Maybe, but we just might have a job here yet, Erin."

"I thought you worked for money, not charity?"

"True, but maybe we can do one and get the other for free."

"You're a real humanitarian."

"Famous for it," he replied as they climbed aboard.

CHAPTER FIVE

The sun was high in the sky, and it felt like a painfully hot repeat of the day before as they soared north towards the town.

"How long you been at this work?"

He turned and looked at Erin's young face.

"Almost as long as you have been in this world."

"You said you have never been a soldier, why?"

"A soldier fights for a cause and for crappy pay. I fight for myself, and my friends. If I am going to run into a shit storm, I want it to be of our own choice, not some arrogant bastard who is happy to have us earn a medal for him."

She nodded in agreement.

"You don't find that morally offensive?" he asked.

"Why would I?"

"Come on. You're an educated and well brought up

young woman. I've never met one like you who wouldn't strike me down for what I do and the reasons I do it."

"Maybe you haven't met the right girl."

He laughed at her response and saw she was semi-serious about the comment. They rode into town and found many of the shops shut, including Kaper's bar. Ryant led them to a centrally located building that was unmarked but clearly represented some kind of town hall.

"Let me do the talking," he stated. "We're going in here to hear them out. We make no promises and take no money from them."

"Why not?"

"Because I want to know what we could be getting ourselves into before committing to anything. Some jobs just aren't worth taking for all the money in the universe."

"I'm surprised to hear you say that."

"Yeah, well, money I like, but my life I like better."

They pulled up outside the hall, and Ryant led them inside to find there were thirty men and women awaiting them. They all stared at Mason as he was led to the front of the room. A man in his late forties was awaiting him with a smile. He wore a well-kept suit and was certainly wealthy.

"This is Nolan Machesky."

"The mayor?" asked Mason.

"No, no," replied Machesky, "I am merely the voice of the local businesses in our town."

"Chosen by the rest of you?" he asked.

Ryant nodded.

That's a start. Somebody they actually want to lead them, Mason thought.

"Not sure what I can do for you, Nolan. My people are gonna be out of here just as soon as get our ship patched up."

"Yes, yes, Ryant has told me. But we have also heard from Mr Kaper about what you did for him and his daughter. We have been looking for someone like you for the last five years."

"Like me?"

"Someone who will stand up to Volkov and his thugs."

"Hey, I just helped them out because I was there, and that's how it went down."

"Please, Mr Mason. Can't you see what is happening here?" pleaded one of the women.

He turned and looked around at the people.

"There are thieves on every world. Seems to me you don't have it so bad. Your trade is going well. You have good clothes and are well fed. You got it better than many."

"Mr Mason," called Nolan, "we are not a charity case. This is not some poor village pleading for help. We only want what is rightfully ours, and we're willing to pay good money for those who are willing to secure that for us."

"Go on."

"The business owners of this town will offer you

ten million credits to solve our problem with Michael Volkov..."

Mason was silenced by the proposition.

"Ten?" he asked.

"Yes, with a down payment of one million to retain your services. We will, however, reclaim our money from your accounts, should you leave with our money before the job is done."

"Hang on. You're telling me your offering ten mil to do this job, and nobody has taken you up yet?"

Nolan shook his head.

It already feels too good to be true.

"And why is that?" he added.

Nolan took a deep breath and began to answer when Mason interrupted.

"No bullshit now. I want the truth if you want me to even consider this."

"Michael Volkov is a very dangerous man with substantial resources. We are offering a lot of money, but at a big risk to yourself in doing so."

He turned to Erin and could see she wanted him to say yes, as did the entire crowd before him.

"I don't take jobs on a whim, and I am not suicidal. If you want us to consider this, you will provide us with an accurate assessment of what it is you want and what we face. Until that happens, I will not commit to anything. Accurate outlines of this Volkov's resources, troops, weapons, vehicles. His allies and threats we are likely to face. I want maps of his facilities, and a history of his encounters with you over the last year. You get all that to me, and I'll talk it over with my crew, but I'm not promising anything."

"Thank you, Mr Mason. I will have everything you asked for assembled presently and dispatched to you this afternoon."

Mason nodded in agreement and walked out of the room. Several of the people patted him on the shoulder when he walked by as if he were their saviour. He continued on and out the door, with Ryant following close behind.

"Ten mil for a protection job. This Volkov ain't no normal bastard, is he? It's bad, isn't it?" asked Mason.

Ryant nodded in agreement.

"I won't lie. You'd have to have balls of solid steel to take the job."

Mason knew that was a challenge, but he would not bite.

"So you'll think about it?" he asked.

"No, I'll have a look over the info, if and when it gets to me, then I'll think about it."

"That's all we ask."

"Mmm," Mason muttered as he turned and left.

"Is that what you were expecting?" Erin asked as they walked back to Mily.

"One of two possibilities."

"How so?"

"When you get bastards muscling in on towns like this, they come in two forms. Loud mouthed arrogant lowlifes who use words and a little violence to present the image of being a real threat, and then there's the real threat. The man who has the knowledge, the resources, and the power to be the son of a bitch the other types only wish they could be."

"And you think Volkov is the latter?"

"The fact he isn't getting his hands dirty doing this is a pretty good indication."

"So what are you going to do?"

"Exactly what I said I would. We'll continue to patch the ship up, and if they get that information to us, we'll talk about it."

"You'd walk away from ten million credits?"

"I'll walk away with my life."

As they boarded the copter, Mason noticed a marshal questioning people in the street just outside the Digger, which was still shut. The man was getting little assistance from the locals, and he already knew what the subject of his visit would be. The marshal turned and glared at them as the rotors fired up. Mason pretended not to see him and pulled away, making a quick but not obviously rushed exit.

"Something to do with you?"

"Surely will be, Erin."

"You make friends everywhere you go, don't you?"

He smiled back with a cheesy grin.

They got back to the ship and found Andrews and Mitchell hard at work. Liu had joined them and left Hella on guard duty, which she seemed to never grow weary of. Liu passed up a component to Mitchell as they came to a standstill beside the landing site.

"Eager to leave, Liu?" Mason asked, jumping from the copter.

"Never wanted to be here to begin with."

"And yet this is where fate brought us," replied Erin.

"Fate? It wasn't fate that shot up our engines."

"Mmm," she muttered, turning her attention to Hella who sat atop the hull of the Foxy Lady. She had a pop up shelter assembled to give her cover from the sun and sat up there in the shade like a statue.

"She been up there long?"

"Maybe since you were gone," replied Liu.

"You think you can trust her?"

"Why, because she has a weird dress sense and tattoos? Her look offend you, Erin?" asked Mason.

"Maybe. She looks on edge, is all."

"You start telling some truths about your existence, and I'll start pushing her for some of hers," he replied.

It shut her up immediately.

"So what did the townsfolk want?"

"About what we figured, Liu. Muscle to help with a

local problem."

"Don't tell me you're considering it?"

Mason looked surprised. "I'd have thought you of all people would want to help."

"Can't save the whole universe. I did my good deed of the week saving this one," he responded, pointing to Erin.

"Your chivalry has no boundaries, I see?"

"We all have boundaries, Erin. If we'd known about this job before we got here, and had time to think it over in the right frame of mind, I'd say it was worth at least a conversation, but I don't like things being thrown in our laps like this."

Mason went quiet for a moment, looking around the barren landscape and thinking it over.

"We'll bring it to the table and discuss it once the sun is down."

Liu shook his head, but he knew he had to accept Mason's command. Mason sat out for the rest of the afternoon, enjoying the sun. He had no clue how to help with the mechanics and engineering required to fix the ship. Finally, Mitchell paced up to him to take a rest. He was dripping in sweat and covered in dirt and dust. He looked down at Mason sitting with his feet up and a cool box of beer next to him.

"I thought you hated this heat?"

Mason smiled. "Turns out it ain't so bad when you don't have to work in it."

Mitchell leant down and took a bottle from the box.

"If you say so."

"How's it going?"

"Andrews has sworn at the old girl more times than I can remember, but he's making solid progress. Tell you what, it's just as well we have him. I've known a lot of engineers, and not many could handle what he can."

"Yeah, well the Boss always knew who was right to hire and who wasn't."

"About that…"

He popped open his beer and took a sip, leaving Mason hanging.

"Well, for God's sake speak up."

He gestured subtlety towards Hella, still sitting under the small half shelter atop the ship.

"Seems a few days ago we had a veteran crew of solid old timers. Now we got two young girls, neither of which will be honest about who the hell they are."

"Well, we all have elements of our past we'd rather not share."

"Maybe…"

"Maybe? Hell you're not even cleared to fly anymore. We break the law every time we fly with you at the con. We all expect to be given a little leeway while we continue to be there for each other."

"And I appreciate that, I really do. The Boss gave me more chances than I ever deserved, but let's not forget why he did. I'm one of the best goddamn pilots you'll ever meet. What have these girls got, beyond a bad attitude and a bundle of secrets?"

"Name one among us who is perfect? That one more than handled herself in that bar. She's got a confidence and resolve like few others. And Erin, she can shoot as good as the best of us."

"You mean you?"

"Yeah, Liu can shoot the same, but never tell him that. Super cop's ego is big enough already."

Mitchell couldn't help but laugh.

"So, yeah, we've got the youngest crew this ship has known since she was fresh off the line, what of it? We expected people to give us the same opportunities when we were that age."

"Don't know about you, but I earned mine. Best pilot of the academy."

"Yeah, you were till you fucked it up, and then what? Boss gave you a chance when nobody else would."

"He needed a pilot, and I was there."

"No, I never told you this, but that day we met, he'd already interviewed three other pilots who wanted the job. You just never knew because you were too late to see them."

"Come on…"

"I shit you not. They were good pilots, all of them. But sometimes you just get a feeling about someone, that they are just…right."

"And this Erin girl? She's gone from a hostage we weren't paid to rescue, to hitching a ride, to carrying a gun."

"We all start somewhere."

Mitchell knocked back his drink because he knew he wasn't going to get anywhere with his current line of questioning. The rest of the day seemed to fly by as they relaxed in the sun, and the time finally came to discuss business. Mason already knew that most there would agree to what he wanted, especially with the sort of money involved, but Liu was the wildcard.

I'm still not sure what to think, but I'm sure willing to give it a chance, unlike Liu.

The crew assembled at the table in the cargo bay. A few extra lights they had gathered from town aided the emergency lighting in letting them see what they needed to. Even Hella had joined them while they waited for Mitchell to bring them the information. They all sat silently for fifteen minutes until he finally appeared.

"They sent everything over?" asked Mason.

"Sure did, Boss…I mean, Captain."

Hella picked up on his mistake and could see the others saw the discomfort it brought him.

"Not earned the title of Boss yet?" she asked him.

"Nothing to earn. The Boss will always be the Boss. I'm Captain of this ship."

"So drab and boring. We'll have to think of a better title for you," she joked.

Felix sat down at the table, feeling rather uncomfortable that he had been the cause of the ruckus.

"All right, so here is everything they sent," he stated, placing a display pad in the middle of the table. He hit a button on it, and within a second, a projection lifted half a metre from the table.

"The town of Melni…"

"That the same town we've been dealing in?"

"Yes, Captain, I never thought to ask either. Just seemed another faceless place we were passing through."

"And now it has a name, it has an attachment," added Liu.

"All right, calm it down," stated Mason. "We have a possible job. We'll weigh up the facts like we always have done. Then we'll make a decision as a crew. Let's do this like we do it. There is money to be made. All we must decide is does the reward outweigh the risk? Felix, you're most familiar with the landscape, you take it from here."

"Melni is a wealthy mining town, population eight hundred and seventy six. They make a shipment out every month that makes them a pretty penny. Despite this, the locally self elected High Sheriff, Colonel Michael Volkov takes at least half of their earnings as a tax, or protection money."

Mason could see Liu was finding it hard to keep up his

hard line. The former detective was starting to feel a little humbled as Mitchell progressed.

"They're being extorted for half their earnings?" asked Erin.

"At least," replied Mason.

"Volkov controls the Sheriff's department and local militia, which combined are believed to total over six hundred personnel."

"Six hundred?"

"Not a lot for a mining world, Erin." replied Mason.

"But a lot for us to deal with," Liu added.

"But…" Mitchell continued, "the townsfolk believe that many of those wouldn't fight against the town, if it came to it."

"That's speculation, not intel."

"No, Liu, but it's information that could be worth knowing, should we take the job," Mason said.

The room fell silent as they took in the depth of the situation. There seemed little to appeal to any of them to make them want to stay there. Mason knew it was the moment to break the most significant element of the briefing.

"This job pays ten million credits," he stated calmly.

It gave them all pause for thought.

"Ten?" Liu asked.

"These miners are rich people being extorted, not poor ones being driven into the dirt," he replied.

Liu could barely believe what he was hearing and turned to Mitchell for confirmation. He nodded in response. It certainly made him reconsider his charitable side.

"Ten mil. Okay, that's more money than this crew had been paid in their life for anything, by a long shot. What do they want for that?"

"They want to stop being robbed," replied Felix.

"And you know what that entails?"

"This isn't going to be a pretty job. Volkov, by all accounts, sounds like a son of a bitch, but we can handle him. We have to do whatever is necessary to stop the protection racket that is going on here. I thought you'd love this kind of work. Make you feel like a cop again?" said Mason.

Liu groaned in response.

"I don't know much about this Volkov, but we both know men like him don't go easily. He's sitting on a lucrative empire here, why would he give it up?"

"Well, surely not by choice, but we aren't in the business of giving people choices."

"Then we face off against God knows how many hundreds of guns and what, hope for the best?"

"You know you can be one cynical bastard sometimes. I'd expect more from a cop, or maybe that's just me."

"Screw you!" he yelled as he reached across the table.

"Stop it!" screamed Erin. She leapt between them and forced them to sit back down. "What the hell are you doing?"

Hella smiled at the whole situation and seemed to find it amusing.

"You find this funny?" Liu asked her.

"Just a little. A cop and a captain slug it out over who has the moral high ground between helping people and making money. What's not to like?"

It was as many words as any of them had heard her speak, and Andrews at least found it funny. They all turned to Erin who seemed to have taken the floor.

"Seems to me this is a whole lot of fighting over a simple decision. A job lies before you, us, and whatever. It pays big with big risks. Take it or leave it."

"Fine words," Andrews sneered.

"Thank you," she snapped sternly.

"Wow," muttered Mitchell under his breath.

Mason kicked back his chair and stood up to pace around the deck while they thought it over. They all looked to him to have the next word.

"You know there's a good chance if we take this job, not all of us will live to see that money, maybe none of us," Liu said.

"Yeah, sometimes the money just ain't worth dying for," added Mitchell.

What would the Boss do? Mason asked himself. He knew his friends were right.

"Okay. This is our business, and we do it to make a

living. If the job risks our lives more than is necessary or acceptable, we have always turned it down."

"Well, not always," muttered Andrews.

Mason looked to him to explain himself, but his lips were sealed. He looked to Hella and Erin.

"When the Boss was here, he always asked for one hundred percent agreement on choosing a mission. I don't see why that should change. Hella, you're on the payroll now, and Erin, whether you like it or not, you're involved in the decisions made while aboard. So, let's put it to a vote," he said, turning to Mitchell first.

"No," he stated after a short pause.

"No," Liu agreed.

Andrews shook his head. "Na, not the smart play."

He reached Erin to see she wanted to say yes, but couldn't bring herself to conflict with the rest of the crew who she owed her life.

"No," she whispered, dipping her head.

He finally turned to Hella.

"Well?"

"Doesn't matter what I think if you need all in to do it."

"Still, I like to know what people are thinking."

"I've been in that town two weeks, and yeah, they could do with some help. But no different to most other places I go. We're in this for the money, aren't we?"

Mason nodded in agreement.

"We're decided then. Patch the ship and get out of

here?"

There were grunts of approval, despite the fact few of them liked the situation.

"Wizard, how long do you need to make that happen?"

"Two days, I reckon we'll be done."

"That's good work. Quicker than you expected."

"Well, I have been getting some help," he replied, glancing over to Liu.

"Never knew you liked getting your hands dirty," said Mason.

"Growing up all I wanted to be was a mechanic, but coming from a family of cops, what are you gonna do?"

Mason took a deep breath and then relaxed.

At least we have a plan now.

"All right. Mitchell, get the cards. It's time we settled in for the night and enjoy the time we have here."

"Hell, yeah!" he answered quickly and leapt from his chair.

They passed out the drinks, and for a couple of hours, forgot the world around them until finally the call came from Hella.

"We've got company!"

Mason jumped to his feet, grabbing his pistol from the table as he did so. The others were close behind him. They could see a few headlights on a solo vehicle approaching from the direction of town.

"Expecting anyone?"

"No one at all, Wizard. Erin, you have that rifle ready," he said, pointing at the one he'd given her. "Rest of you, too."

"Trouble?" asked Andrews.

"Not that I know of, but I'd bet good money this isn't a social call."

He stepped to the edge of the ramp and looked up to where Hella's voice had come from. He couldn't see her, for she sat on top of the fuselage with no lights at all.

"Hell? You keep an eye about us. This might not be our only guest."

She suddenly appeared at the edge, with her thick jet-black hair draping over the opening.

There's still something that doesn't feel right about her. She seems all too familiar with my way of life, but I don't understand how.

"It's the Sheriff. Nobody else is with them."

"How can you be sure?"

"I'm sure," she replied resolutely, as if there were no reason to doubt her.

"Well, okay."

He couldn't understand how she could know that much when to him it was just a blur in the distance. The vehicle got within a hundred metres, and in the limited moonlight they enjoyed he could see there were no obvious weapons or armour attached. It was a lightweight skimmer with ducted fans and a small crew of maybe two or three. It was indeed as Hella had said, the Sheriff's vehicle. He holstered his pistol and adjusted his gun belt.

"Lower you're weapons, but keep 'em close to hand!" he yelled to the crew. He turned back just as he thought it over. "And for God's sake don't shoot them unless there is no other choice."

He didn't want to pick a fight, but he'd always be ready for one. The Boss had taught him that.

The skimmer came to a quiet stop but kicked up dust into the hold of the ship that wasn't appreciated by any of them. Mason spat out the mouth full of dirt over the side of the ramp as they got out.

"Captain Mason?" the first asked.

They stepped into the dull light emanating from the cargo area of the ship until he could make out their faces. The man wore a crest on his chest that he assumed denoted his position. The three all wore matching black dusters, but shared nothing else in common. One carried a rifle in his hands, the other a scatter laser. The man in the middle with the crest was empty handed, but Mason could see his coat flaring out slightly at the thigh where he carried a pistol.

"What can I do for you?" he asked without responding.

"You are Captain Mason?"

Mason sighed in response. The formality bored him.

"I'm the captain of this ship," he replied, just to irate them.

"I'm Sheriff Alken. I believe you passed me in town

earlier today."

"I was in town today, but you don't look all that familiar."

They both knew he had seen the Sheriff, but he wouldn't give him the satisfaction of admitted it. He'd avoided the man for a reason. Alken was in a fit and healthy shape, and younger than he would have expected in his position. He was of a similar age and build to Mason, though the Captain still towered over him because of the ramp he stood on. Alken was clean-shaven and well kept. He had the look of a lawman who led a comfortable life with little strife.

"There was a shooting in town yesterday, and I'm investigating it at present. Word has it that self-defence was the nature of the death."

"And?"

"And we'd be inclined to log it as such, if those involved were to not take it further and departed without any more trouble."

Mason did not respond.

"You see what I'm getting at, Captain?"

"I get it," replied Mason in a drawn out and unimpressed manner. He stepped slowly down the ramp to the Sheriff and stood before him.

"My crew landed down here without intention. Our engines were shot to hell, and we went into town for parts. Now since then, a few folk have asked if we could help them out here. We gave it some thought and decided it wasn't for us."

"Glad to hear it, Captain," the Sheriff replied with a smile.

"That was until you turned up here and tried to tell us how it is."

The smile turned to a frown, but Mason continued before he could reply.

"I don't especially like cops. I like corrupt ones even less. You came here to flex your muscles. Well I'll give you a little advice. Next time you try and do that, make sure you can back up your tough talk with more than a couple of apes like these boys you brought along."

Alken took offence to his words, threw his coat aside, and reached for his pistol, but he wasn't quick enough. Mason leapt forward and placed his hand over Alken's to stop him from drawing. He quickly head-butted the Sheriff in the nose, forcing him to stumble back and lose grip of his weapon. Hella then appeared out of the shadows above them and landed on the rifleman. She wrapped her legs around his neck, levered him back, and flipped him over so that he landed hard in the dirt.

The third man swung his scattergun around, but as he did, Hella grabbed a rock from the ground and threw it with perfect accuracy so that it struck him on the back of the head. His body twisted by the sudden impact, and he fired a single shot that sent laser scatter bursting into the open sky. The scene was lit up momentarily as if a flare had gone up until the laser blast quickly faded away.

Mason stepped up to Alken and pressed his foot down over the man's hand as it rested on the grip of his pistol.

"I wouldn't," he stated.

Alken looked up at Mason's right hand hung beside the pistol on his side, ready to draw at a moment's notice. He finally submitted.

"All right!"

Mason removed his foot and let Alken fumble around in the dirt to get to his feet.

"You've made a big mistake here, Mason! Attacking an elected sheriff and striking his deputies."

"Actually, Alken, what I saw is you draw down on us to do us harm, and that's exactly what those cameras will confirm," he said, pointing up at the landing cameras above the ramp.

The Sheriff shook his head as he patted dust off his coat and looked up at the cameras.

"Goddamn it. You're not welcome here, none of you are. Stay out of town. Stay out of all of our lives, and get your asses off Krittika!"

The three of them retreated cautiously and sheepishly. Mason knew he'd made another enemy in the Sheriff, but he was at least relieved that blood had not been spilt. Their vehicle fired up and tore off into the night without another word from any of them.

Mason turned to see Hella had gotten to her feet without

so much as a single sound. She continued to impress him in the most surprising ways. He nodded in gratitude for her work. She was calm, as if it had meant nothing to her.

"Cameras, Captain? You know those haven't worked for two years?"

"Yeah, but the Sheriff doesn't know that, does he?"

"You really dislike cops so much?"

"You haven't worked that out by now, Liu?"

"You like me," he smirked.

"Think he'll be gone for good?" asked Mitchell.

"No," replied Liu, "I've known men like him. He's firmly in the pocket of this Volkov character and has made that quite clear. He'll ensure he keeps pressing us till we're gone."

"And if he takes this to Volkov?"

"He won't, Erin, not yet. He'll fear Volkov's wrath the same as the townsfolk and will do everything he can to manhandle us off this world by himself."

The Sheriff's visit left a foul taste in Mason's mouth, and he knew the others felt the same. He didn't like being pushed around by anyone, but the fact he knew the town's people were experiencing it daily made him angry.

"I'm gonna call it a night," Andrews said. "I want all my energy for tomorrow to get started at first light. Let's be out of here before trouble comes back to our door."

CHAPTER SIX

Another night had passed, and Mason awoke having slept for just a few short hours. It felt as if they had been on Krittika for weeks. He had spent a lifetime getting used to weeks of travel aboard a star ship. But that was life without outside influence. The situation they had landed in was pulling him in all directions.

It feels like we'll never get off this world until some duty we've been chosen for is complete.

The sun was coming up, and he was the first awake. There was no sign of anyone being on guard duty. He suspected they'd all gone to bed having been content they were now safe. The Sheriff's trip had been weighing heavily on him all night. It was the final element to tip him over the edge. He hadn't met Michael Volkov yet but already knew he would hate him.

Mason lifted his bed up where it was hinged against the

wall and pulled out his gun roll. He carried it out, dumping it in the back of Mily where she was laid up in the cargo bay.

"Going somewhere?" a faint voice asked.

He looked up and saw Hella's silhouette on the ramp.

"Jesus, do you never sleep?"

"Only when I need to."

He shook his head and lifted a box of ammunition from one of the side racks.

"Crew agreed, and you're going ahead with the job anyway?"

"We agreed not to do this as a crew. I'm going alone."

"Why?"

"Maybe because I can make a difference?"

"Not that you just want ten millions credits for yourself?"

He stopped to think. The prospect had not crossed his mind.

"No, not for the money."

"And yet when you asked me to join this crew, you told me you do what you do for money."

"Yes, I did, but maybe there's more to life than that."

"Then join the Army," Liu stated.

He turned around to see the crew were rising from their rooms, and Liu had stepped out to address him.

"What?" he asked.

"You always said you join the Army to fight for a cause,

not for the money. Sounds like you've just become the perfect candidate."

"Hey, I just want to help these people. Is the idea so strange to you? Have you stopped being a cop for so long you've forgotten what that's like?"

His comments did shame Liu a little as he thought back to how vehement he was about not taking the job.

He climbed into the driver's seat of the copter, but Mitchell stepped out from his room to block his path.

"Move."

He shook his head.

"You're not the only one who's had the night to think this over, Max," Liu said.

Mason turned back in surprise.

"People are trying to push us around, poke us, and prod us. That's not how this crew works. Time we put the boot down."

Andrews staggered out of his room. He was still in his dirty clothes from the last two days' of work and looked exhausted. It was obvious he had been listening to all that had gone on.

"Well?"

"Captain, the fact you were willing to go it alone against all odds is enough to convince me. We're with you, all of us."

Erin stepped out of her room carrying the rifle he had given her in her arms. She nodded in agreement also.

"If we take this offer, we're in to the very end. It's gonna get ugly, no doubt."

"None of us have ever expected this job to be a walk in the park," said Liu.

"We aren't going to let you do this alone," Mitchell added.

He nodded in appreciation.

"Like you all, I thought long and hard over this. Up till last night, I could have left this world and put it to the back of my mind. But Volkov sending the Sheriff here to talk us to death, well he just went and pissed me off."

"Poetic," replied Erin.

He smiled in response and then turned to Andrews.

"I want you to continue your work here. We may not be leaving anytime soon, but having the Lady up and running could really turn things around when things start to heat up. You'll have to go it alone, though."

"No problem. Give me today and maybe a bit of tomorrow, and I'll see what magic I can work."

"I need one to stay here and keep guard." He turned to Hella. 'You seem to like it, fancy the job?"

She nodded in agreement, "Whatever you say, Boss."

"I'm your boss now, but I'm not THE Boss. You can call me Max, Mason, Captain, Sir, but never Boss, you hear?"

She nodded in acceptance.

"Yes, Boss."

It's clear she has a real problem with authority, but it's a character flaw I can live with.

"The rest of you, gear up. The time for playing nice is over. Armour, rifles, let's be ready. We're going into town to take this job."

The group leapt into action. Within five minutes, they were climbing aboard and raring to go. Mitchell was at the controls with Mason riding shotgun. He raced Mily forward.

"Hang on!" yelled Mason.

Mitchell brought them to a stop on the ramp where Hella stood.

"You need a gun?" he asked her.

"Managed so far without one," she replied dryly.

If it were anyone else he would assume arrogance, but she had already proved herself more than once.

"Well if you do, feel free to grab one. You'll find a few rifles and pistols in locker three, back towards the bridge."

"I'll be sure to use whatever is needed."

"Right, let's move!"

They raced off down the ramp and over the sun baked hard ground north towards the town.

"Think the offer still stands?"

"I thought you weren't in this for the money, Mitchell?"

"I didn't say I didn't want it, Captain."

Mason agreed. It would be a couple of years' salary for each of them at least.

They rolled into town to find it was operating as normal. Several of the passersby recognised Mason and stopped to stare at him as they rode past.

"Where we heading?" asked Mitchell.

"I've no idea where Machesky can be found, so head for the Digger, and we'll go from there."

He turned back to look at the others.

"Town's people are friendly, but there are plenty residing nearby who aren't, so keep your wits about you."

They pulled up to the bar to find the Sheriff's copter parked outside. As their engines fired down, they could hear a voice shouting inside the bar. Mason leapt off the copter and rushed through the doors without a weapon in hand.

"Who fired the gun?" he heard a voice yell. Mason passed into the dark room and found Alken with his hands around the barkeep's throat and forcing his back against the bar. He shook his head in disbelief, feeling sorry for the poor man who'd taken two beatings since they'd arrived.

"Who did it? Who did it, Kaper?" he screamed into the man's face.

"I did!" Mason shouted.

Alken's head snapped around at the sound of his voice.

"Well, well. Back in town, looking for trouble again. Well, you've found it."

He released his grip on Kaper. He took a wide face on

stance to Mason and pulled his coat back from around the pistol slung at his side. Mason could see the grip of the laser weapon was carved out of some kind of bone. It was a lavish and unnecessary show of wealth from a lawman.

Alken stood five metres from Mason, and he showed no attempt to close the distance. After the humiliation he'd had the night before, he was being sure to stay at draw distance. Mason could hear his people stepping up to the edge of the building outside and listen in. They were awaiting his next move, as they could see Alken from the windows.

"So, here we are. You just admitted to the murder of a man in town; a man who was in the employ of and undertaking Mr Volkov's orders. I'm the Sheriff, you're the murderer, and you've got a gun. Drop it and come quietly, or I'll have to do this the hard way," he said with a sleazy grin.

Mason wasn't intimidated and only carefully studied his opponent. He let Alken sweat a little. He hadn't seen Mason use a weapon, and that uncertainty was clearly unnerving.

"Not a murder. I put down a dog, and it seems to me, I stand before another one. You either pull that pistol or give it up."

Alken's eyes squinted as he frowned. He realised Mason wasn't joking and quickly reached for his gun. Mason's hand grabbed his own pistol in lightning speed, and it was aimed at the Sheriff before his gun was out the holster. Mason fired just a single shot. It hit the pistol and launched the smashed weapon out of his hands. The Sheriff cried in pain from the burn of the blast. He cowered down, holding his wounded hand. Mason slipped his pistol back into his holster, and Liu stepped into the room to join him.

"Glad I never met you when I wore a badge, Captain."

"You won't get away this this, Mason!" screamed Alken.

Mason strode up to the Sheriff who cowered down as he approached. He grabbed him by the collar of his coat and hauled him towards the door. Erin was nearly thrown aside as the door flew open, and Mason rushed out, launching Alken out into the road headfirst. He landed hard and slid to a halt on the concrete ground. His cheek was badly scraped and bleeding from the abrasion, and he was almost knocked out cold by the landing.

"I see your face around town again, and I'll blow your head off, you hear?"

Mason suddenly realised how quiet the street had gotten. He looked up to see the shopkeepers across the road had come out to watch, and all who were passing were frozen and fixated on him.

"Okay! Okay! We'll take the job!" he roared at the top of his voice.

Applause broke out which echoed all around the buildings either side of the street. Kaper came out from the bar to join him.

"Thank you, Captain. You don't know what this means to us."

He turned around and responded softly.

"Ten million about?"

Kaper nodded.

"Well how about that?"

"Please, take a seat in the bar, and I'll get Nolan to join us."

He looked back and watched Alken scurrying off with his tail between his legs. He crawled onto his copter and tore off with all haste.

"Looks like you made a friend," said Mitchell.

"He's not the first last asshole we'll meet here," he replied. "You stay out here and keep watch."

"Oh, come on, you know how good their beer is."

"But we don't," Liu said and stepped inside.

"We brought some back for you the other night," Mitchell protested.

Mason stopped beside him.

"I don't expect we'll see any trouble too quickly, but be ready."

Mitchell calmed down and took up position by the door.

"I'm a pilot remember, not a fighter."

"Well, you ain't got no ship to fly, and you can't repair engines for shit. So make yourself useful."

"Nice," he muttered.

Mason went inside, and Kaper was already pouring out drinks for them all.

"Should you be drinking when you could have to fight and shoot at any time?" asked Erin.

"Probably not," he said, taking a glass from the bar and sipping from it, "but this isn't the Army. Calming everyone down a little right now can't do any harm."

Two minutes later, Machesky rushed through the doors. He strode up to Mason and shook his hand.

"Thank you, Captain," he said and went around them one by one and did the same.

"We haven't done anything yet."

"Oh, but you have, Captain. Herschel was a leech, and Alken too. You've just dealt with two problems we never could."

He looked back to a young man who had come with him and was waiting at the door. Nolan gestured for him to come forward. He took the case and opened it, presenting it to Mason.

"One million credits. A down payment to show you how serious we are."

Mason reached down and placed a hand on the bag, but Nolan didn't release it. Instead he leaned in close to whisper to Mason.

"Just remember what its for, ey?"

He stood back and Mason responded at normal volume

so that others could hear.

"We take money for a job. We do the job. Unless we die trying, we'll succeed."

Nolan nodded in gratitude and sat down at the nearest table, gesturing for Mason and the others to join him.

"You've seen what we face here. How do you expect to go about putting our problems to a stop?"

"Well, I haven't met this Michael Volkov, though I do intend to. But I can already tell you that he won't go easily. He's making a tonne of money off your backs, why would he ever want to stop? Men like him need to either be put in their place, to such an extent they never again step over the mark, or you kill them."

Nolan recoiled at the idea.

"What? What did you think you were paying us for?"

"To negotiate for us, to stop the people of this town being extorted."

"And what do you or we have to offer to bargain with for this? Money won't do it because he'll always want more. There is nothing you can bring to the table to make him stop."

Nolan looked at Erin, for she seemed the most civilised and understanding of them all.

"You think we hired you to murder him?"

"Murder? No, that isn't our business," replied Mason.

"He's right," said Erin. "This Volkov needs to either fear coming near you, or he'll never stop."

"How can we achieve this?" asked Nolan.

"You can't. You leave that to us."

He could see Nolan was getting more and more anxious.

"Yes, yes, but what are you going to do? If you just scare him a bit and then leave, what is stopping him coming back the month after?"

"Which brings us to the other possibility as I have already said. We aren't here to uphold the law or to negotiate a peace. We'll get you what you have paid for, however that has to be done."

"Captain Mason, I cannot endorse you killing Volkov, no matter what kind of man he is."

Mason sat back and thought for a moment before taking in a deep breath. He leaned over the side of the table and picked up the case full of money. He threw it over at Nolan who almost fell off his seat to catch it.

"I thought you understood what has to be done here, but if you want to carry on as you always have, then you can keep your master and your money."

He was taken aback by the sentiment and was still in shock. Mason could see now that Nolan had expected from the very beginning that he could simply hire some muscle to intimidate Volkov into changing his ways. Mason stood up and pointed his finger at the businessman.

"You need to get your head screwed on right unless you want to keep living under his thumb." He turned to Liu. "Come on, let's go."

"Mason!" Erin called out to him.

He looked at her and shook his head. Erin looked back to plead with Nolan.

"You are letting your only chance walk away."

"All right!" he shouted.

Mason stopped, waiting for him to continue.

"You know these situations. I don't. I still can't condone bloodshed though, not unless it is in self-defence."

"Then I think you can't have spoken to the rest of the town's people anytime soon. When I dragged Alken out of the bar not fifteen minutes ago, those people were waiting for me to finish him off. If I'd have put my gun to his head and pulled the trigger, it would have been met with applause."

"And that is how you do business?"

He stormed up to the table.

"Let me be absolutely clear. If we take that money, we do it my way. I don't know your trade, and you don't know mine, so what'll it be?"

"Captain Mason!"

The cry was loud and came from outside the bar. It was a deep and booming voice. An authoritative tone that told him it wasn't going to be anyone friendly.

He looked at Nolan and saw the fear in his face.

"That's... Sergeant Hunter."

"Who's he with?"

"The militia. One of Volkov's men. He won't be alone.

Alken must have summoned him."

"In the last twenty minutes? How far are they stationed from here?"

"Two hours' drive. They must have been passing by."

"Just our luck," he replied sarcastically.

"Kaper, this place got roof access?"

"Yes."

"Show Liu the way."

"Why?"

"Just do it!"

"What are you doing, Mason?"

"Nolan, that sergeant has come here to cause trouble. Just like always. It's time to take a stand. Only question you have to ask yourself, is do you want us to take this job or not?"

"Do I have a choice?"

"Probably not."

"Then do whatever you have to."

"What was that?" Mason asked for clarification.

"You do it... your way."

Mason smiled in response. "Well, okay then."

He paced up to Erin. She held her rifle close but was obviously worried.

"Never shot at a person, have you?"

She shook her head.

"First time for everything. I need you to cover me from that window. You don't fire unless they do first. Stay inside and keep yourself safe. Got it?"

She nodded in agreement. "What are you going to do?"

"I'm gonna go and see what all the fuss is about," he replied confidently.

He adjusted his gun belt and stepped up to the door, pulling it back slowly so as not to cause anyone to react. He stepped out to see four militiamen. They all wore dark green jackets and matching short peaked caps, with sun protectors hanging down over their shoulders. Metal insignia was pinned to their chests, but he couldn't make it out. Besides this, none of their equipment was uniformed with a variation of weapons, webbing, and bags.

The first thing Mason noticed was that two of them held Mitchell between them as a prisoner.

"Sorry, Boss."

"Not your fault."

The militiamen were coated in dust and looked weary from travel. He could see Alken skulking in the background under the shade of one of the shops.

"You are Captain Mason?" one of them asked.

"Sergeant Hunter, I assume?"

"That's me. Sheriff Alken here tells me you've been causing some trouble. We don't like trouble in this town or any other in our district."

"Glad to hear it, Sergeant. Me and my boys here had some engine troubles and only came for parts."

"Were that the case, you'd have already have been on

your way by now. I'm thinking you were paid to be here."

Mason couldn't deny it; for despite it not being their intentions, it had been the way it worked out.

"Word is you killed a man here in town, an offence punishable by death, but I also hear no witnesses have yet been found. Pack up and leave this world, or I'm sure those witnesses will come forward. Neither of us wants any trouble here."

"Yeah, Sergeant, that's a real good deal, but how about this one? You give me my guy back, and I won't blow your head off."

"Now, Sheriff Alken said you'd be one to make threats like that, and yet his head still sits atop his body."

"For now," Mason answered calmly.

"Okay, let's try this again."

He grabbed Mitchell, pushed him to his knees, and held a pistol to the side of his head.

"We've already got one of you. We'll take him with us and try him for the unlawful killing of Herschel, then we'll come back in greater number to take however many of you are stupid enough to still be here."

Mason squinted as he tried to get a read off the man and see how serious he was. Everything he was seeing told him he had to act.

"Sorry, Felix."

"For what?" Mitchell replied; sounding confused.

Without hesitation, Mitchell snapped his weapon from

its holster and fired from the hip. The laser hit Hunter square in chest, but he got a shot off as the impact struck. A laser from the pistol clipped Mitchell's ear before striking the ground in front of him. The Sergeant was launched off his feet and disappeared from view. The other three men lifted their weapons to respond, but one was struck a second after Mason had fired. The laser came from the roof and hit one of their shoulders. He was incapacitated and immediately on the ground in pain.

Mason fired the next shot and took out the leg of one. Liu struck the last in the face, killing him instantly. The doors of the bar flew open, and Erin rushed out to Mitchell's aid. Mason was ahead of her and got to the bodies to see Hunter was gone. He saw the Sergeant vanish down a narrow corridor between two of the buildings in front of him.

"Help him!" he yelled as he gave pursuit. He took the bend he had seen Hunter disappear down and could tell by the speed he was making, the laser had made little effect. Mason guessed he must have been wearing the same torso body armour they wore, expensive gear for the average militiaman.

He heard a tussle around a bend and rushed as quickly as he could. As he took the bend, an arm struck out from the corner and clotheslined him. It sent him into a roll, and he crashed down into the dirt with no finesse. His pistol flew out of his hands in the fall. He tried to get to his feet, but Hunter kicked him to the ribs hard. He rolled over onto his back from the impact. His armour saved him from broken ribs, but it still hurt like hell.

"Guess you're not all that, Captain," said Hunter disdainfully.

Mason rolled over and got to his feet as quickly as he could. He reached for his knife, but his hand found an empty sheath. Hunter lifted the weapon and brandished it with glee, having ripped it from him during his fall.

"Looking for this?"

Hunted lunged at him with the knife with lightning speed. Mason leapt back and pulled in his stomach to avoid the strike. He stabbed again and Mason parried the strike and grabbed the knife hand, trying to get a lock. Hunter skilfully twisted out, and the knife was thrown from both of their hands. Mason realised he was fighting a skilled opponent, more so than he had in a long time.

He punched forward with a quick jab, but Hunter moved up and under the strike. He drove a knee in, took a standing grapple, and forced him back into the sidewall. Hunter's elbow struck Mason's face and crunched his neck. He recovered quickly with a punch to Hunter's face and a second into his ribs. The Sergeant came right back at him with two furious rib shots. As Mason responded with a hook, the Sergeant took hold of his arm and launched him over his shoulder so he landed on his back.

Two laser pulses rushed overhead and struck the wall

beside them. Hunter looked up. Liu was rushing towards them with a gun in his hand. He turned and fled rapidly as Liu arrived at Mason's side.

"What the hell happened to you?"

"Got into a fight."

"Looks more like you got your ass kicked!" Liu shouted and rushed past.

"Thanks!" snapped Mason.

Liu got to the edge of the building and saw a vehicle rush off into the distance. The Sergeant was at the controls and already two hundred metres out. Liu lifted his rifle and took aim. Liu fired a single shot that zipped past his head. He fired another, but the vehicle was beyond his range, and he couldn't see if it had struck its target or not.

"Get him?" Mason asked. He was hunched and nursing his ribs.

"No."

"Well, I guess we both failed."

"He'll go right to his boss with this. We're gonna have a whole world of trouble bearing down on us."

"That was always gonna happen once we took the money. Now it'll just be sooner rather than later."

"Nolan really thought this could be settled with a stern conversation. He must have come from one polite planet."

"Liu, when you work with scum on a regular basis, we can forget there are some good people out there who are oblivious to the more ugly sides of life."

"You're right, and even if we can take this Volkov character down, they're gonna have to learn to fend for themselves."

"One thing at a time."

He went to go back to the bar, but Liu stopped him.

"Volkov has numbers on his side, you know if any of the people in this town will fight with us?"

"Even if they would, how useful are a bunch of untrained civilians?"

Liu knew he was right. They turned and paced back to the main street. Mitchell was being led into the bar. He was able to walk, despite the pain. They followed them through and sat down at the table they had been talking at before the fight. Nolan sat there with a tall drink and looked astonished.

"Is there really no other way?" he asked.

"Sometimes, you just have a fight on your hands whether you want one or not."

"And if we just forgot it all and continued to pay everything Volkov asks of us?"

"It's too late for that," Liu said. "Now you've insulted him and brought into question his authority, he'll want to make an example of you all."

"What does that mean?" asked Kaper.

"It means that a few assholes wanting to take your daughter for a bit of fun will seem like nothing compared to what they have in store now," he replied.

"Why have you brought this upon us?" Nolan asked.

Liu could see Mason was at first silent in shock, and then the anger began to build in his eyes, so he stepped in to calm the situation.

"You didn't ask to be robbed in the way you are, but you did recruit us to solve it. You recruited a team of - I hate to say it, hired guns to solve your problem. You can't have thought for a moment this was going to end peacefully?"

"I hoped," replied Nolan wearily.

He turned to Mitchell who was getting bandaged up by Erin and Kaper's daughter. He was knocking back spirits and grimacing at the pain. Liu stepped over and snatched the glass away from him, the bottle too.

"Hey, I need that!"

Liu shook his head. "Same old same with you."

"That's not fair. I'm in pain!" he yelled.

Mitchell looked to Mason for help, but it did not come.

"You're not the one that got shot!" he shouted again.

"No, we're the ones who saved your ass. We got a big problem to deal with. None of us can afford to get drunk, no matter how bad they are hurt."

"I told you I wasn't cut out for this shooting stuff. I'm a goddamn pilot."

The room fell silent until Nolan finally broke it as he took another sip.

"Maybe we hired the wrong people."

"No," replied Mason. "You hired the only people who

would take this lousy job. Now man up, and deal with it."

He strolled back to the door and looked out across the street where they'd recently shot the militiamen. A few of the town's people were now back on the street, but they avoided the bodies like the plague. Liu joined him.

"They want the problem solved, but they don't want to get their hands dirty."

"Are you surprised?"

"I don't care who they were, Liu. They don't deserve to just be left out there that."

"Maybe we should cut our losses now, and get the hell out of here?"

"Too late. We took the job and started it. We're in this now till it's done."

"And if it costs us our lives?"

"You're one cynical bastard, you know that?" replied Mason sharply.

"You know back when I was a cop, before I was a detective, I saw this kind of thing all the time. Maybe not on this scale but the same thing, some thug muscling the locals about for money, or whatever. More often than not, we would try and take them down and fail. If the victims are too scared to help, then what chance do you have?"

"Well then, I guess it's time they got their act together."

He turned around and paced up to address Nolan."

"There are three bodies out in the street there. Get them sorted."

Nolan looked at a loss for having been told what to do.

"On your feet!" Mason ordered.

Nolan almost jumped out of his skin and stood up. Mason grabbed his shoulder and led him out towards the door.

"Look at them!"

"They're dead."

"Not the dead, your people. Passing by like the bodies are litter on the sidewalk."

He shoved Nolan forwards.

"Get it sorted!"

Nolan looked sheepish, and Mason could see he was desperate to find an excuse not to, but Mason's eyes told him not to try it. He staggered over towards the bodies and called over a few people by name to help him.

"It's a start," Liu said.

CHAPTER SEVEN

Thirty minutes had passed as they watched from the bar with the door prised open, the town's people clearing the bodies. It had dawned on them all that they had taken a job beyond their means.

'So what now?" Erin asked Mason.

"What do you mean?"

"I can see what you're thinking."

He turned out of curiosity to look at her.

"Oh, and what might that be?"

"You're thinking Volkov is going to come back with an army that you cannot expect to face."

He recoiled. "So what's the answer?"

"You took the job and the money, and you said you always see things through, so leaving is out."

"And?"

"And you're looking at them and thinking they don't

have a hope in hell of being useful in a fight."

Mason turned to Liu.

"Hell, girl, where are you from?" asked Mitchell.

She rolled her eyes at the pilot.

"It doesn't take a genius to see what is going on here. So that about sums it up?"

"That's the problem, but what's the solution?"

"Find people who can shoot and who are willing to join us, Mason."

"Us?" asked Liu.

"I'm here with you, aren't I?"

"Are you? You didn't pull the trigger when the time came against those militiamen."

She dipped her head in shame.

"Can you remember the first person you shot?" Mason asked Liu.

"Yes."

"How easy was it for you?"

He went silent.

"Go on," said Mason.

"Like I said, we need more people who can handle weapons and fight."

He lay back in his chair and thought about it for a moment.

We've never recruited during a job before, and it's far from ideal.

He looked to Liu for an opinion.

"It's not a bad idea, but where could we hope to find

anyone?"

"Frontier world like this, bound to be a few who could be up for it."

"Good luck finding 'em."

"A small town like this always has around three bars; an upstanding one like this with nice furniture and expensive drinks. A family friendly place to take the kids, and then there is the dive. The sort of bar where your boots stick to the floor, the beer costs half as much as everywhere else, and half the patrons are ready to kick your teeth in. That's where we'll find a few guns to join us."

"And you think you'll find a place like that in this little town? Come on."

"Damn right I do."

He turned and called for Kaper to join them.

"What can I do for you, gentlemen?"

"We're looking for a bar."

"You're in one. With the finest wines and ales and the best food in town."

"Yes, yes. I want a different kind of bar. Where in town do all the fights start? The place with the cheapest drinks and the rowdy customers gather?"

He shook his head. "No, no, you don't want to go there, Captain."

"No I don't, but I still asked."

He looked around to see if his daughter could hear and then leaned in close.

"The place you describe is called 'The Slap Up'."

Mason sat back and smiled.

"But really, Captain, you don't want to go there. It's full of dirty gambling, fights, and whoring. This is a good town, and it's the only stain on its name."

"So you do have more vices than expensive alcohol?" he asked with a smile.

Mason kicked back his chair and stood up sharply.

"Where you going?" asked Erin.

"Not where am I going? Where are we going? Liu you hold down the fort here while Mitchell sobers up. Erin, you and I are going on a recruiting trip."

He could see Kaper wasn't happy about it at all, but Erin hadn't heard what he had said and happily joined the Captain.

"So where to?" he asked Kaper.

"Captain? Surely not."

"Just tell me where to find it, and we'll be on our way."

"Get to the crossroads south, and then head west for maybe five hundred metres."

"It's on the edge of town?"

"Thankfully, yes."

"All right, let's go."

They stepped out, and Erin looked surprised he didn't go for the copter.

"Half a click and you're walking? I haven't seen you walk anywhere in the time I have known you."

"Well, maybe you don't know me as well as you thought. Which gets us back to you."

"What about me?"

"Liu said you didn't fire when Hunter and his men started the fight. He wasn't wrong."

"I…"

"I know what you did. You hesitated. Back at the ship you proved to us you can shoot, but in this line of work that doesn't count for anything, if you can't do it when it's needed."

"Then why did you defend me?"

"You know you did wrong, but Liu isn't always the most accepting of types. If it were up to him, we'd only recruit highly training ex military and law enforcement. That would rule me out for a start, let alone you."

"I just don't know what happened. I just couldn't pull the trigger when it was a person in my sights."

"Then we're gonna have to sort that out. It's a dangerous job we do, and you're getting thrown into the deep end. If you're gonna be a part of this crew and get your fair share of the cut, you have to do your fair share of the work. I need to know the next time you need to shoot someone you won't hesitate. Hesitate, and you could get one of us killed."

"Maybe I'm just not cut out for this kind of thing."

"Maybe, but right now you're flying with us, and we need all the help we can get."

"This is normal life for you, isn't it?"

"No such thing as normal. Every job is different, and the only dull day is the journey from one to another."

"So you enjoy it, then?"

He thought about it for a moment. It was not something he had ever considered.

"It's all I've ever known. Boss recruited me young, just like you have come to us. I wouldn't know how to do anything else."

"So you keep doing it because you don't know what else to do?"

He nodded. "Maybe. But I wasn't born into any money, and working a desk wasn't for me. Just sort of fell into this, what's not to like?"

"Maybe the fact that people are trying to kill you on a regular basis?"

"And yet you didn't choose a dangerous life and still ended up in the thick of it?"

It gave her pause for thought.

"So you haven't told me where we're heading. Kaper didn't seem to think it was a good idea."

"If we always did what the barkeep recommended, where would we be in life?"

"So we're heading for another bar?"

"What makes you think that?"

"Because he wouldn't be so anxious about you leaving for any reason but a rival establishment."

"You're quick. You might just work out for this team yet."

The sun was high in the sky, and there was little shade as they made their way west through the streets. Transports continued to roll in and out of town at a steady rate, with workers and materials aboard. Sweat was dripping down their faces, and their clothes were soaked.

"Must be close now."

Just as she said it, a woman flew out into the street and landed hard in the dust. Another rushed out from the side of the street, and a fight ensued. Erin stopped. They watched as several men poured out onto the street and clapped and cheered as they watched the scuffle.

"You're just going to stand there and watch?" Erin asked.

"Hey, it ain't my fight."

"Asshole," she muttered and rushed forward to help. She reached the two to pull them apart but was struck in the face by the back of one of their hands, throwing her onto the floor. The small crowd roared with excitement that she had joined the fight. She put her finger to her lip and found blood trickling from her mouth. Erin got to her feet, got the rifle from her back, and fired a shot into the air. The single laser shot made a loud crack which echoed down the long street and made them all stop in their tracks.

"Enough!" she screamed.

The two women looked at her and immediately turned back and kept slugging it out. Mason stepped forward and grabbed Erin by the shoulder, hauling her towards the door as the cheering continued.

"Why didn't they stop?"

"Why would they? Look at you. You were never going to shoot them. They'd swallow you whole."

She looked up to see the name of the bar.

"Seriously?"

"It's the right place for us."

"How?"

"Trust me. It was your idea to recruit for guns, so here we are."

They passed inside and were met by a wall of smoke from pipes of what must be a local herb they had never encountered. It was everything Mason had described as what they needed. Erin looked around in disgust at the appalling state of the bar. It looked like a brawl had taken place the night before. It was the middle of the day, and yet there were more than thirty customers lying about the room.

"How can we find anyone of any use here?"

"To survive a bar like this, you've gotta have something," he replied.

Nobody registered their presence.

"I bet a good few here are travelling through. Pilots and smugglers, the lower end of the miners and workers."

"You make it sound like home."

"Well, to some people it is. Can't say I wouldn't hold up in a place like this myself for a few days."

"To what, drink yourself to death and catch God knows what off those poor women," she said, pointing to what were obviously the bar's own prostitutes.

"Spend a few weeks on a ship with nothing to do, you'll be amazed how appealing a place like this can be."

"I'd take your word for it, but I can't say I'm convinced."

"Yeah, well maybe if you grow up getting everything you ever wanted. To the rest of us, this is a good time."

She ignored the comment and carried on as they stepped towards the bar.

"You think we'll really find good people in here?"

"Hell, no, but I've seen more fight in these people than I have the rest of the town. Good people aren't always what it needs to get the job done."

They reached the bar. There were two huge vats behind the barman and no sign of anything else to choose from. He looked like he could have been the evil twin of Kaper, same height and build. But he had a few scars on his face and a carefree look about his face.

"Light or dark?" he asked them.

Erin looked confused. The barmen turned and pointed to the two huge vats. She looked along the bar and saw every customer drank from an acrylic mug with either a blond of brown mud-looking colour drink.

155

"I'll… pass."

"You want to work this life, then you need to experience the perks," Mason laughed. He turned back to the barman.

"Two of the dark."

"Could have at least gone light," she replied.

"What?"

"It's hot, a time for white wine."

"I'm sorry, did I offend your carefully honed drinking etiquette?"

The barman passed over two mugs, which were chipped and rough but at least looked relatively clean. The fluid they contained was a thick muddy brown colour with a frothy head and to Mason looked perfect. He took a tip and smiled.

"Pretty solid stuff."

Erin took a careful sniff of the top of the glass, recoiled and placed the mug back on the bar. Mason laughed at her response and turned to have his back against the bar so he could study all around him. Several of the miners still wore their work clothes and were most likely catching a midday drink during their lunch break. An old music player of a sort he hadn't seen in twenty years was propped up in the corner, but looked like it hadn't worked for some years.

His eyes panned across the room until he stopped on one character who stood out. The man sat alone. He must have been six feet tall and had a deep scar on the side of his temple that ran up into his hairline. He had a squarely carved jaw and a well-built body, but on the outside of his legs was some kind of exoskeleton device. It was slimline and connected at three points on his legs as well as his hips. Erin could see Mason staring at him.

"Alvertron exolegs, impressive," she stated.

He had never seen the technology before and was surprised to hear she had. He looked at her for answers.

"It's high tech equipment, the very latest. It'll allow even somebody without working legs to walk and work the same as the rest of us."

"That come cheap?" asked Mason.

"No, not at all."

Mason studied the man carefully. He held himself like a soldier, and had pride and confidence. He had a pistol held in an expensive fix lock polymer holster on the side of his exoskeleton legs that were subtle over his cargo trousers. He was sitting against a wall, so he could see all that went on. Mason could tell he carefully studied all around him, despite doing everything he could to hide the fact.

"That's a good start."

"A crippled soldier, how'd you figure?" she asked.

He was taken aback.

"I thought you'd be more understanding to a man of disability."

"Understanding, yes, but we're looking for fighters."

"And you said those legs will work as well as ours?"

"Most of the time, yes."

"Well I don't see a whole load of other candidates around here."

She looked around for alternatives. Many were drunk, a bad sign at that time of day.

"Let's go."

He gave her no choice, so she followed him to the stranger's table.

"Mind if we join you?"

The stranger looked at Mason and was unimpressed, but when he noticed Erin standing at his side, he changed his tone.

"Buy me a drink and you can take a seat beside me."

Erin quickly offered up her drink that hadn't been touched and placed it before him.

"Anyone would think you'd arranged to meet me here."

The stranger's jacket was off, and his shirt was fairly close fitting and clung to what was clearly a well-defined muscular physique. It was clear he was in great shape before whatever caused him to lose the use of his legs.

"If you're with Hunter, I'm still not interested."

"Now why would you say that?" Mason asked.

"Because he's been trying to recruit me for the last three months."

"That how long you have been here?"

He nodded in agreement.

"Well we aren't with the Sergeant. In fact, we got into a little altercation with him this afternoon, and he left in a bit of a state."

"Bullshit."

"It's true," Erin added.

"Really?"

They both stared at him sternly, hoping he would accept their news. Instead, he looked over to the bar and yelled.

"Hunter been caught up in a fight in town here today?"

The barman nodded.

"Something over in the main street. Last I heard, he was running from some new guys in town!" the reply came.

The stranger looked impressed.

"Well, you have my attention. Hunter is a son of a bitch. About time somebody gave him what for. I'm Vincent… Hughes."

"Captain Max Mason, and this is Erin."

"Just Erin, nothing else?"

She shook her head. "Does there need to be?"

"So what can I do for you?"

"A group of concerned locals has hired us to sort Michael Volkov out."

Hughes recoiled at the proposition.

"Maybe we came to the wrong table," said Erin.

Mason smiled as he could see she was working an angle against him. He took in a deep breath before getting started on the beer she'd donated him. Mason continued.

"We're getting ten mil to take on Volkov. You join us and prove yourself useful, and you can expect a three percent stake in the profits."

He looked at the two of them carefully and spoke to Erin.

"That what you're getting?"

She fumbled as she tried to respond. Mason jumped in before he could carry on.

"She'll be getting standard rate for the ship's crew, five percent. I'm asking you in for a single job."

"And if I die during this job?"

"Well then it doesn't matter, does it?"

"So you must have some idea I am right for the job?"

"You know how to wear a gun. You have been monitoring this room since we got in. You have the strongest defensive position. You're ready to defend yourself at a moment's notice and you clearly served."

"Most perceptive, Captain; Staff Sergeant in the VASI Second Army. You a soldier yourself?"

"Nope, just a man with a gun who wants to make some money."

"Really, because you look more like a man of principle to me? Nobody would take the job of fighting Volkov for any price in the world. And then there's you," he said, looking to Erin.

"A mercenary wouldn't have such a pretty girl working as an equal in this job."

"Maybe I just like to be surrounded by pretty things."

He looked around at their surroundings and smirked.

"So you need to wear those things all the time?" asked Mason.

He was pointing at the man's exoskeleton. The struts of the device were just a couple of centimetres thick, with joints at the knee and foot and a power source at the waist.

"If I want to stand," he replied. "Rest of the time I'm on wheels. These legs have solar recharging. In a sunny environment, I can get up to twelve hours out of these babies, enough to get a job done."

"As long as you don't have to stay in the field."

He took another sip of his beer.

"Captain, if you came to a bar on this little world looking for hired guns, then you must be desperate. I'm all out of credits and have nowhere left to go. I was honourably discharged for medical reasons due to injuries sustained. The money I got from the Army didn't come close to covering the medical bills. These legs blew my pay out, and now I'm just as desperate as you. So you say you'll give me three percent of the money to fight for you. I say, let me sign up for the long haul and take the full five."

He lifted his glass as a salute, knocked back the thick liquid, and slammed the glass back down on the table. Mason sat back and thought about it for a moment.

"Tell me you have many other choices?" he continued.

He's right. He's a wreck of a man, but the best hope I've found yet of a useable ally.

"Those legs of yours, they going to cause us any

trouble?"

"None, I can be as good as any man for most of every day."

"And the rest of the time?"

"Running on wheels. But you can't tell me you need me on my feet every hour of every day?"

"You be honest and fight hard, that'll do."

He stretched out a hand, and it was quickly accepted. They could both tell Hughes was taking the job out of desperation. Neither of them could see he had any hope of getting anywhere on Krittika. He had the look of a man trapped on a frontier world having expended the last of his wealth.

"When do we start?" asked Hughes.

"Right now. Militia under the control of Sergeant Hunter kicked up some trouble in town today, and we sent 'em packing. It won't be long till they come back in greater number. Have you got weapons?"

"I haven't got much more than you see me wearing."

They were the words of a desperate man. Erin gained respect for Mason for taking him in, but Mason only saw a trained gun hand that could be helpful.

"When do we leave?"

Mason looked around the room. He saw little potential for further fighters to join them.

"You know anyone who would want in on this deal? It's damn dangerous, but the payoff is great."

"I can't say I made any friends here. Even on a world like this, the Alliance has a lot of influence."

"And yet you are here?" he asked.

"War is over for me. I gave everything I had to give. Now its some other fool's time to do so."

"You really believe that?" asked Mason.

"Why is it any concern of yours?"

"Because the war goes on. But for us, we fight for each other. We must trust each other and be there for the crew. Can you do that?"

"Yes," he replied sternly.

"Then you're hired. No pay up front, no benefits, or perks. All I can guarantee you is a fair share of decent pay should you survive and do your job."

Mason lifted his glass and Hughes did likewise.

"All right, grab your things. We're heading out," stated Mason.

Hughes grabbed a holdall from the seat beside him.

"Ready."

They were both astonished.

"This is why I didn't join the Army, Erin."

They knocked back the last of their drinks and made a move for the door when a ruckus broke out ahead of them. Two men were thrown aside as several others erupted into a vicious fistfight. A monster of a man seemed to be fighting all the others. He was six foot five, with a shaved head, and a scar that ran from his cheek down his neck and into his shirt.

Furniture crashed aside the hulking man until he drove three men out of the door into the street with a chair. Mason took the opportunity to pass through the mayhem and open door to the street. As they got into the daylight, they could see the lone man clubbing three others to near death with the chair. Erin looked to Mason as if she expected him to stop it, but he seemed more entertained.

The barman ran out into the street with a gun. Mason stepped in and pushed it aside, causing the laser pulse to crash into the dust. The lone man took his opportunity to break the jaw of one and throw another aside. The street went quiet.

"You want to deal with him that's your choice!" yelled the barman. He got a grip on his weapon and retreated into the bar.

The man shrugged off the dust from his coat and kicked one of his victims in the head while he lay helpless on the floor.

"You want a job?" asked Mason.

The stranger looked suspicious but not at all concerned.

"What does it pay, and what do I have to do?"

"Five percent of ten million credits of this job and all others we get while you work for me."

"You only answered one question."

Mason realised the stranger was not one who could be toyed with.

"It's dangerous. Fight Volkov and free this town of his hold on it."

"What are you doing, charity work?"

"Last time I checked, you don't get ten mil for doing charity," replied Mason.

Hughes stepped in closer and leaned into Mason's side.

"This man is a common thug, how can you expect him to care?"

"People care for enough money."

The man had overheard the conversation and took a few paces closer to look at them all. His hand rested on the grip of a pistol carried across his belt. He studied them both carefully until he finally got to Hughes. He spotted a pin on his collar immediately.

"You served with VASI?"

"Until this happened to my legs."

He spat out on the floor.

"I assume you didn't?" Hughes asked.

He looked down to see his pistol had the unmistakeable bird's head grip used only by the Alliance gun factories on Griswold.

"Then you must have been Alliance, unless you stole that gun."

Mason was impressed at Hughes' perception as he had not noticed that himself. The man seemed to wear it with some pride, and they could both see the hatred in the eyes for the VASI pin Hughes wore.

"So that was issued to you," stated Hughes, "and clearly nothing is stopping you fighting. So you're either AWOL during a war, or a deserter, which is it?"

"It's none of your goddamn business is what it is."

He turned to Mason as he could see he was the leader of the group.

"So who do you fight for?"

"Ourselves. I'm Captain Mason, and this is some of my crew. We pissed Volkov off, and he's gonna be coming for us soon. Do you want in?"

"You're not seriously going to hire this thug?"

Erin looked wary of him, but Mason knew they needed capable fighters at any cost.

"Well, Captain," said the stranger. "You are heading for a fight, and you've got what, a cripple and a little girl, you're not selling the idea to me."

Taking him on board hardly seems like the best idea. He's a crude brawler and doesn't look like he can be trusted, but he seems to be the only chance we have of another fighter and he's slipping away.

"What are you doing on this world, stranger? You're not a miner. Not a dealer, or a soldier as it would seem. What are you doing here?"

"Thinking that's none of your business," he replied, tightening his grip on the Griswold on is belt.

"Whoa, all I am saying is, what is here for you? I'm guessing you don't have a flight off this world, and there aren't any other jobs worth you taking. How you gonna keep paying for those drinks and a bed?"

He loosened his grip on the pistol as he thought it over. He had the look of a man who'd lived in the same bar for the last few weeks.

"Fight with us, and you'll get a fair share of the profits, a room, and a crew to have your back."

"And if I don't want it?"

"Fight is coming to town, whether you like it or not. You might get tied up in it either way. This way you get a payday out of it."

"And her? She taken?" he said, gesturing towards Erin.

She took offence at the idea of being a commodity and opened her mouth to speak when Mason stopped her.

"Erin is one of our crew. She might not look all that much, but she can shoot, probably better than you."

"Mmm," he muttered.

"On the bright side, she'll be something pretty to look at when you work with us."

Erin coughed at the thought, but Mason turned and nodded for her to calm down. She knew he was working an angle, but she didn't like it.

In all honesty though, because she's pretty is part of the reason I allowed her to stay aboard, he thought to himself.

The man grumbled as he ogled the young woman, smiled, and then rubbed his hands together, thinking of the money he was being offered.

"I'm up for a fight."

"I thought as much."

Hughes looked highly offended, and Mason knew it was a conflict they may never settle.

"Now, both of you. I never signed up for the war and don't have an awful care for either side. Sometimes, we'll get work from either party, so you're just gonna have to deal with that. Whatever conflict may have been between you, you need to let it be. You both take this deal, then you work for me and put all that crap aside?"

Hughes accepted, and the stranger spat on the ground and ignored it.

"Name's Viktor, and I can't say I care much for the war either. You pay me and give me a bed, I'll shoot anyone you want me to."

"Long as that stays to killing the right people, we got a deal," replied Mason.

Viktor nodded and followed them back towards Kaper's bar.

CHAPTER EIGHT

Liu looked surprised to see Mason walk through the door with two new faces that were clearly fighters. Mitchell was still complaining as he knocked back the local root based soda.

"This is Liu and our pilot Mitchell."

"Vincent Hughes," he replied, and reached out and shook their hands.

Viktor stayed back and seemed to care little for instructions.

"That's Viktor."

"Both these guys signed up?"

"What, Liu, you doubted I'd come through?"

"No, Captain, I just wasn't sure you'd find anybody crazy enough to sign on."

"Maybe not in a pussy place like this," muttered Viktor.

Kaper wanted to disagree, but he could see Viktor was

not a man to cross.

"So what now?" asked Viktor. "We taking this fight to the man?"

"No, no need. He'll come to us."

"He turned, strode over to the bar, and pointed for a drink."

"This is no time to be drinking," insisted Hughes.

Viktor ignored him. The others looked to Mason to do something, but he knew he could not risk causing a rift among such a newly formed team.

"Can I have a word with you a moment, Captain?"

"Yeah, sure, Liu."

They stepped outside beyond the hearing of the others.

"This is no good. We're going into one of the most dangerous jobs of our lives and taking on newcomers we know nothing about."

"Tell me we have a choice?"

"What?"

"You're telling me what isn't ideal. I'm asking you what can we do different?"

Liu didn't have any answers.

"Can't just call for backup on this one."

"Maybe we can. Put out a bulletin and try and get some of our old contacts on board."

"Old contacts? Near enough everyone who has ever worked with us is either dead or retired."

"But it's got to be worth a shot?"

"We can try, but in the meantime, we need to get down to the job. Come on, time isn't exactly on our side."

He led Liu back inside where the rest of them were awaiting his command, except for Viktor who had settled down with his drink.

"Here's the deal. Volkov is gonna come for us with whatever he can muster. We are going to hold here in the town where we have cover and the support of the locals. When he comes, we're gonna offer him peace, or give him the gun if he refuses."

"That's it? That's the plan?" asked Erin.

"What else would you do?"

"Seems a bit basic. Hunker down and wait for him."

"Sometimes the simple plans are the best ones. Mitchell, I want you back at the ship to help Wizard with his repairs."

"I ain't no mechanic."

"No, but it's either you or Liu goes, and you suck with a gun."

Viktor chuckled to himself in the corner. Mitchell took offence, looking to Mason to do something.

"Hey, don't look at me. Learn how to handle yourself, and I'll stop ragging you for it. Now, when you get back to the ship, I want you to send Hella our way with all the extra ammo we have. We'll need her here in the fight."

"What about protecting the ship?" Liu asked.

"Fact is it can't fly, and once we've taken all the weapons and ammo, there really ain't much that can be robbed. We

171

need to amass all our firepower here if we expect to have a hope in hell."

"Your sympathy is overwhelming," Mitchell murmured.

"Come on, man up. You got clipped. It happens."

"And who's fault was that? I should never have been in combat."

"Well, maybe you wouldn't have been if you didn't get the ship shot up," said Liu.

"You mean I shouldn't have saved all your asses?"

Mason jumped in between them and stopped them from coming to blows.

"Hell of a crew you have here," said Viktor.

Mason shook his head in disbelief.

"Look, we've got a big fight on our hands and the chance of a big payday. Let's work together and get this done. Mitchell, take Mily back to the ship and get to work helping Wizard. The rest of you, it's time we started planning this defence!"

Mitchell winced as he got to his feet and rushed out from the bar to do as ordered, cursing words as he did.

"Kaper, I need that map of the town!"

The barman jumped to their assistance and brought over a tabletop projector. He hit the on switch, and it displayed a metre square overhead map of the town.

"So, which direction are they going to be coming at us from?"

"Volkov's mansion is to the east way past Avery's place.

He has the militia base nearby. That's where he'll come from."

"Assuming he hits us head on."

"We have to take an educated guess to some degree, Liu. We can't account for all eventualities."

They went silent, and he looked over to Viktor. He still sat alone with his drink.

"You want to get in on this?" Mason called to him.

Viktor shrugged his shoulders, got up, and dragged his chair over to join them.

"He'll hit with a pincer movement from the north and south, with a minimal force from the east to draw our eye," Viktor said.

"How'd you figure?" asked Hughes.

"Because he has help from within the Alliance forces, and that's exactly what an Alliance officer would do when opposing a hostile town of militia."

Mason could tell Viktor wasn't any ordinary soldier, and he was curious to pursue the subject, but there was no time for it. Hughes seemed to be nodding in agreement.

"You think he's right?"

"As much as I hate to say it," he responded.

"Nothing from the west?"

"No, that would be over extending and cutting off their retreat."

Mason was surprised to hear such military knowledge. Despite being a fighter his entire life, he was rarely involved in a stand up fight. Their team relied on surprise attacks and assaults that meant they could study their enemy's positions before going in. Now they were almost on the other end of the scale.

"Okay, and we could expect to face up to two hundred armed fighters."

Hughes recoiled in shock, but Viktor didn't respond at all.

"So, ideas?"

"This how you do things around here, sit around and brain storm?" asked Hughes.

"Clearly you weren't an officer," replied Liu.

"What?"

"Someone has to plan an operation. Maybe you were used to just doing what you were told, but in this business, we are the officers, the generals, the grunts, and everything else."

"So let's try this again," Mason sighed.

"Explosives," Viktor answered.

"Go on."

"This is a mining town. They must have tonnes of explosives lying around."

"Yes, that's a start," Liu agreed.

"We're in the middle of the town, do we want to blow the whole place to hell?"

"It's a good idea, Hughes. We can set all kinds of charges that could even the odds," replied Mason.

"And if we do blow a few shops apart?" asked Hughes.

"This isn't a poor town. Get rid of Volkov, and we save them enough money to fund any manner of rebuilding within a month's pay."

Several hours went past as they debated the matter and had the locals gather all the supplies they could think of. Hella finally walked into the bar, grabbing the attention of both Hughes and Viktor.

"Where the hell have you been?"

"Nice to see you too, Captain," she replied.

"No, really, you could have been here hours ago," added Liu.

"Felix needed patching up, and Andrews was having a hard time working alone."

"So you do engine work?"

"I do all sorts, Captain."

"Really?" Viktor grinned.

She turned to the hulking man with a despicable look.

"Who the hell is this?"

"Best man you'll meet on this world," he responded, to the sound of groans from the others.

She strolled up to Viktor who seemed enthralled with her. She rested a hand on his thigh that made him smile. He looked up into her eyes and just as he did, felt the tip of a knife on his throat and froze.

"You're the new goon, great. More to fighting than size."

"Not my experience," he whispered back.

She pushed the blade in just a little more so that she broke the skin and blood trickled down his neck, but it didn't get the response she wanted. He didn't respond to the pain and only smiled. He quickly grabbed the blade of his knife in his hand, without regard for the edge and threw her back. She was launched across the bar and into a tumble but managed to nimbly roll back onto her feet.

Hella rushed at him with immense speed and knife in hand, but his pistol was drawn and pointing at her head before she'd closed the distance. She leapt into a roll to get under the barrel of the gun, jumping up to him with her knife on his groin, but stopped as she felt the barrel of the gun on her temple.

"Enough!" Mason shouted.

They both lowered their weapons, and Hella stepped back.

"One big happy family," said Liu, shaking his head.

Mason could see Kaper. He had heard everything and was behind the bar, stunned. He could see the man wondered if they'd hired the wrong people and condemned the whole town. The Captain got to his feet, scowling at the team while be paced up to the bar owner and his daughter, who seemed even more in shock.

"Don't worry."

"Don't worry? Look at you. You're a bunch of crazy people. You're more likely to blow this town up and turn on each other than deal with Volkov!"

He looked back to the team. They were all looking at him for answers. In the past, the Boss had always dealt with such matters. It was his time to step up now as much as he didn't like it. He turned around and responded to Kaper in a calm voice of a volume that could be heard by all.

"You're a family here. Not just you and your daughter, but the rest of this town, right?"

He nodded in response.

"Okay, and despite the fact this town works together, it's not always fun and games, is it? Tell me you never argue about anything?"

Kaper was thinking about it and couldn't answer.

"You see! Our crew is just the same. We're dysfunctional. What do you expect? We're expected to risk our lives for a living on a regular basis. We get the job done. That's what we're paid for, nothing else. We aren't paid for our manners, not for keeping our language clean."

The barman was thinking it over carefully and looked at his daughter, remembering how Mason had saved her. Viktor broke the silence, burping as he sipped back on his beer. Mason could not help but smile.

"We aren't perfect, nobody is. You might have wished for the proper authorities to do the work for you, but they don't care. We're here, and we're willing to risk our lives for an amount of money that is sizeable, but not worth dying over. It took a lot for us to except this job, and we were within hours of leaving you to deal with this yourselves. Now we're in, and we're not perfect. We don't have much in the way of gentlemanly conduct."

Kaper reached down beneath the bar, and Mason's instinct was to think he was reaching for a gun. He carefully pulled his pistol from its holster, holding it ready to respond, when Kaper's hand came back up with a tankard of ale and presented it to him.

"I really pray you are everything we hope you are. And while you are working this job, feel free to drink here at no charge, but I won't have such terrible language used within these walls in the presence of my daughter and the rest of our customers."

* * *

"This isn't working!" Mitchell hollered.

Lubrication fluid burst out over him. He spat it out and tried to keep it out of his eyes. He pulled himself across the floor and sat back against a sidewall, staring at Wizard who had given up too.

"The fit isn't right here at all."

"What, these assholes given us the wrong part?"

The two of them looked at the new coil they were trying to fit, and the old one that was in two parts and lying on the deck where Andrews had stripped it.

"This for the wrong engine?" asked Mitchell.

They both were quiet, trying to figure it out.

"You think Mason getting us into this job is a good idea?"

"I don't know, Mitchell. You have been to town and seen it all. I've just been here. All I know is the price, and it's dangerous."

"Come on, man, you were at the briefing."

"Yeah, and it just seemed like another job to me."

"Another job? We're talking about facing several hundred trained soldiers, and we have no ship to rely on to get us the hell out of dodge."

"Like things usually go perfectly? Way I see it, we didn't choose to be here, and we're here till these repairs are complete. Rest of the crew may as well work and get us some money."

Mitchell fell silent. A moment later Andrews had a moment of clarity as he stared at the coil they were trying to fit.

"It's a different part."

"I know. I've been telling you that for the last ten minutes!"

"No, it's the right model for this ship, just newer than our blocks here. I bet they're a new model. Can't be a whole lot different."

He got to his feet and staggered over to where the twisted parts of the old coil lay, picked up one of the fragments, and returned to Mitchell.

"Look, the basic component is the same. It's just this reinforcement ridge that has been added. We cut that off, and the baby will slide right in."

"You sure about this, man? I mean right now we can go back and maybe exchange it. We start fucking with it, and God knows."

"Come on, when have I not known what I was talking about?"

"Maybe if you'd spotted this damage a little earlier, we wouldn't be on this shithole planet at all."

Andrews shook his head in disbelief.

"When we talked about this mission, you were all too happy to be working for that ten million credits."

"Well it's easier to like the job up until you get shot," he replied.

"Fetch me the tools I need to get this job done, and maybe you can be in the air before you know it."

"Mason has got us in for the long haul here. We might be airworthy tomorrow, but we ain't going anywhere."

"Don't know about you, but I'd at least like to have the option."

"Yeah, yeah, all right. I'll get you the tools. Don't break anything now while I'm gone."

Mitchell staggered to his feet. He had almost forgotten about the pain in his ear now for all the sweat dripping from him. Without any climate control, the ship was like a sauna.

"Goddamn you, Mason, sweating my ass off for this job."

He passed through the engine bays towards the cargo hold where their power tools were held. The table in the middle of the room was still filled with cards and empty cups from their game. For a moment, he wished it could be all over, and they'd just be continuing that game.

"Some things just ain't worth the money," he said to himself.

He went to the racks of equipment and pulled out a cutter when he noticed a shadow cast over him. His heart almost stopped, and he turned to see three armed men stood on the ramp of the ship.

"Felix Mitchell, you are under arrest."

He looked at them for just a moment, and then turned and ran as fast as he could. Two lasers smashed into the bulkhead, and the men pursued him. He reached the cockpit, slammed the blast door shut, and sealed it. The three men began hammering on the door, but he knew they didn't stand a chance of getting through.

Mitchell collapsed down against the doorway. He didn't even know what they wanted, but he knew it couldn't be good.

"Mitchell, we have a warrant for your arrest! Open this door and come peacefully!"

He'd been in enough trouble in his life to know he

didn't want to go with any authority. He had spent time behind bars, and he couldn't bear to do so again.

* * *

Mason grabbed his glass, lifted it in gratitude to the barman, and took a sip. He had a simple policy against drinking when on a job, but it would have been rude to refuse. As he did so, his comms unit crackled, and Mitchell's voice sounded out.

"We're under attack. We have fucking intruders aboard. I repeat..."

They heard laser blasts over the comms as it cut off. Mason's face turned to stone as he realised their vulnerable ship had come under attack.

"This is Mason, what the hell is going on?"

The comms was silent until Mitchell finally replied in a calmer tone.

"Three guys got aboard. They've got guns, and they say they have a warrant for my arrest."

"All right, stay calm Mitchell. Listen to me carefully. I need to know everything about these guys."

"Just get here and sort them out!" he screamed.

"We're coming, but I can't guarantee we'll make it in time. So do what I say."

"All right," he said in a quivering tone.

The comms went silent again for a moment, and the

crew in the bar waited with baited breath to hear the news. Only Viktor seemed to show little care and continued with his drink as he had done before.

"They've got dusters like the Sheriff wore, and badges."

"Right, you hold on tight. We'll sort you out."

Mason leapt to his feet.

"Liu, Erin, Hughes. You work on securing the town's defences. Viktor, you're with me!"

"Finally some action!" he replied.

* * *

"I ain't coming out, and you can't force me!" Mitchell yelled.

He looked through the small piece of reinforced glass of the door that divided them.

"I am Deputy Rondel, and this here is a warrant for your arrest. Now you can either come peacefully, or this is gonna be messy!"

Mitchell shook his head.

"I haven't done anything that gives you the right to come after my ass. Whatever charges you've made up, I ain't biting!"

The Deputy studied the door carefully. They both knew the weapons they carried couldn't get through it. One of the others stepped up to Rondel and spoke.

"We aren't gonna get through that."

Mitchell smiled. "That's right, boys. Blast doors. My friends with big guns are on the way. When they get here, you better be long gone!" Mitchell shouted and broke out into laughter.

"His buddies are in town. We got twenty minutes maximum to get him out," said Rondel.

"I can't see how that could be possible."

They all went silent for a moment, and Mitchell was delighting in their loss, but the smile was wiped from his face with the Deputy's next words.

"When we came in, I saw some parts on the ground and work being done; tough for a single guy to work on a ship like this. Probably at least another guy on board, find him!"

"No, no, it's just me here, you hear!"

Rondel pointed for his two colleagues to sweep the ship. Mitchell knew it wouldn't be long until they found Andrews. He lifted up his comms.

"Mason, you need to get here quick!"

"We're on our way!" the call came back.

Only a few minutes later, they hauled Andrews up to the door of the cockpit. His face was bloodied where a pistol grip had been smashed into his face. Mitchell looked away.

"Mitchell!" Rondel shouted. "We came here for you. This man means nothing to us. Come peacefully, and he will not be harmed!"

He didn't respond, but he heard them hit Andrews

across the face a second time.

"Mitchell, you come here and look at your friend!"

The pilot edged to the window. He didn't want to see, but he couldn't give up on a friend. A gun was pointed to Andrews' head.

"We will do whatever is necessary to take you into custody. That could include killing this man. His death will be on your hands, as he is of no interest to us!"

One of the men struck Andrews again, but it didn't seem to change Mitchell's mind.

"We haven't got much time," one of them said to the Deputy.

Rondel lifted his pistol and held it to Archibald's leg.

"You come out or I fire, three, two, one."

Light flashed and he fired. Andrews screamed in pain as the laser passed through his upper leg. Mitchell turned away and put his back to the door. He didn't want to see any more.

"Mitchell! We have five minutes left. That's all the time we need to finish your friend here. Next shot will be his other leg, then his arms, and then his head. It's your choice!"

There was silence. Eventually Rondel rested his pistol on Andrew's other leg.

"This is it, Mitchell. The other leg! Three, two, one…"

The door lock slid aside, and Mitchell pulled the door open. He looked down at Andrews who was reaching breaking point.

"Thank you," he muttered through the pain.

Rondel reached forward, hauling Mitchell through the door and over the wounded Andrews. The Deputy stopped to deliver a message to the Archibald.

"You tell your Captain his pilot is being arrested for flying commercially while banned. Flying under the influence of narcotics, flying without logging flight plans with the Alliance, and negligence at the control of a vessel."

"Narcotics? What? I've been clean for years."

"Oh, yes, I almost forgot."

The Deputy quickly lifted up a metal syringe and plunged it into his neck before he could respond. Mitchell stumbled back as the drugs quickly took effect, and he was helpless to fight back.

"A terrible thing, flying under the influence of hard drugs. He'll be shipped off world for sentence. Mr Volkov says to tell you that you can all leave here if you wish. Lay down you're weapons, and you will be given safe passage to the nearest IPA facility."

Andrews spat out blood before going eye to eye with the Deputy.

"You picked the wrong crew to tangle with, son."

"No, you picked the wrong planet to come down on. Get your asses out of here, or you'll be buried where you landed."

They turned to move, but as they passed, Andrews took a hold of Mitchell's arm.

"We'll come for you, I promise."

Mitchell grumbled but was out of it from whatever had been pumped into his system. The deputies hauled him away and out of his grasp. Andrews knew he was helpless to do anything else. He only took relief in the knowledge that Mason was on the way. He could hear their vehicle racing off into the distance, but it was another twenty minutes before he heard another approaching. Two sets of footsteps rushed inside, and he prayed they were friendly this time.

"Andrews? Mitchell?" Mason called.

"Here!"

The heat of the laser had sealed the wound, but it still hurt like hell. Mason rushed to his side to assess how bad it was.

"What the hell happened here?"

"They took Mitchell on a flying violation. A Deputy Rondel."

"You fight back?' Viktor asked.

Andrews turned and looked at the towering man he didn't recognise.

"Who the hell is that?"

"Say hello to one of the two new crew we hired. This is Viktor. He's a bit of a son of a bitch, but you'd be thankful for having him in a fight."

Viktor smiled, appreciating the description. Mason reached down and hauled Andrews to his feet. He carried him to the cargo bay, sitting him down on one of the chairs where they had played their card game. The old hand was close to silence, despite his injuries.

"I shouldn't have left you without protection."

"Oh, quit that sorry bullshit. You couldn't know this would be their play."

Viktor looked down at his wound, lifting part of the ripped fabric of his trousers up to see where the laser had struck his thigh.

"I've had worse."

"That's really reassuring."

Mason leant over to look. "We're gonna have to get you to town."

"My work isn't done here."

"Ours either, but something tells me we aren't leaving this world anytime soon. You need medical attention, and you aren't doing any work in this state."

"We used to leave men in your state to the enemy."

"And you wonder why I never signed up, Viktor," Mason said.

Mason grabbed the medipack and wrapped the wound quickly. There was little bleeding from the laser blast, but he needed to keep the wound clean during their journey. Andrews had little feeling or control in the leg. He hauled him to his feet and carried him over to the copter.

"Get the rest of our ammunition, Viktor."

"Would if I knew where. First time I've been on this hulk."

"Hey!" Andrews shouted. "Nobody talks about the Lady like that."

"The Lady?" he asked, looking around the ship. "Looks more like a well worn whore."

The two of them stopped and glared at Viktor.

"She's called the Foxy Lady, and if you expect to get off this world anytime soon, you'll start respecting her," stated Andrews.

"Wow, okay. Didn't think anyone ever got so attached to a lump of metal."

Mason pointed at the Griswold on his side.

"You put any value on that lump of metal, or would you sooner trade it in for something a little sharper?"

Viktor's hands shot down over the grip of the pistol protectively, turning it slightly away from them.

"Nobody touches my Martha."

Mason smiled in response as he protected the gun like his own child.

"Little sentimental there?"

"Me and Martha have been through a lot together."

"Now you know how we feel about the Foxy Lady."

Viktor drew out his pistol, which gave them both pause for concern, but he simply held it out in his two palms and looked upon his beloved Martha. It quickly sparked a world of memories. He finally looked up and around the interior of the ship. It was as weathered and full of character as his Griswold was. He holstered his pistol again and smiled. It seemed he found comfort in the ship.

"So this place is my new home?"

"If you survive the mission, and we get her flying again."

"Don't know about you, but I intend to survive to spend that ten mil."

"Five percent of," Mason reminded him.

"Yeah, yeah, of course."

Mason got the distinct impression he was not a man to be fully trusted, but he was also the best fighter they'd find who was willing to help.

"You think you can see yourself working with us?"

"You keep getting jobs that put money in my hand, and I can see this working."

Mason helped Andrews up into the copter.

"He's Alliance, isn't he, Captain?"

"How'd you know?"

"A gun like that, and you see his belt buckle?"

Mason looked back and could see a heavily worn steel hexagonal buckle. It was standard issue within the Alliance.

"Where on earth did you learn to recognise those two things?"

"I've been alive a little longer than you, Captain. You learn things along the way. He's not still serving, is he?"

"I figure he wouldn't be down here getting drunk and looking for work if he was."

Andrews grimaced. "I don't like it. Guy like that could really screw us over if he saw the chance to take us for everything we have."

"So he ain't completely trustworthy. That's the life we lead."

"The Boss would never have hired anyone like him."

"Yeah, well, if the Boss was here to help, maybe we wouldn't have to."

Andrews couldn't argue with that. Mason got down from the copter and headed for the lockers.

"Over here," he called for Viktor.

Viktor stopped as he sore VASI stamps on some of the ammunition crates. Then he turned to see Alliance ones beside them.

"You buy from both sides?"

"Doesn't mean anything to me, and it shouldn't to you either. You aren't fighting for anyone but yourself anymore, are you?"

He said nothing.

"So you still feel allegiance to the Alliance?"

He shook his head.

"Maybe I did once, but when your own boss shoots you in the back, it makes you think."

Mason suspected he meant it literally, but he wasn't going to pry.

"And yet you still wear that, and carry that gun."

"You think I'm gonna buy a new belt when this one still does the job? And Martha, nobody gets their hands on my girl."

"Well, okay, then."

He grabbed two of the boxes and pointed for Viktor to grab the others. They threw them aboard and climbed in. Mason rode the copter up to the entrance, hit the door close button, and raced out as the ramp began to lift. Andrews watched the hatch slam shut.

"That ain't gonna keep a determined thief out."

"I'd be more worried about scavengers stripping the metal," Viktor laughed.

Andrews looked over to Mason in horror.

"Let's hope we have a ship to come back to," he said.

"I'd be more worried about getting back with our lives."

CHAPTER NINE

They arrived at the town, and Andrews was treated to the finest of care, but Mason saw the fear in many of the locals' faces when they saw the second member of his team injured. Andrews was laid out on one of the tables in Kaper's bar. They had now been given rooms there upstairs. Liu was leaning up against the front door, looking out at the town going about its business. Mason went up to him. He could see concern overshadowed the former detective, but Liu spoke first as he approached.

"They're scared, Max. Look at their faces. Frightful of what's coming next. They could be helping to reinforce and defend their town, but they have already resigned themselves to accept defeat. Doing what they always do is all they know how."

"How would you feel, Ben? We're a step behind them every time, and we may have given more than we got, but we can afford far fewer losses."

"And what about Mitchell?"

"We can't just leave him."

"Can't we? He's a junkie and always will be. Maybe we're better off finding a new pilot?"

"No way, aren't you forgetting who saved our asses on Sharini?"

"Don't let that go to your head. Doing your job right sometimes, doesn't excuse your fuck ups the rest of the time."

"You think you're being fair? I know how you feel about his habits, but he's been clean a long time now. Either way, we aren't leaving him to their mercy, and that's final."

"They're just buying time to gather their forces," Viktor joined them.

They turned to see the hulking fighter had crept up on them and had been listening in. He lit up his pipe to a look of disgust from Kaper. The barman wouldn't speak out, but neither would Mason.

"Why?" asked Liu.

"Because by now he's probably realised who he's dealing with. I've heard of your crew before. The Captain's name was different then, but I know about a few of your ops. If I heard that along the road, Volkov will know it by now. Your reputation is for going in hard and fast. Surprised you haven't to be honest."

"Well, you aren't as dumb as you look."

He grinned at Liu and puffed smoke out from his pipe.

"But they could also be using it to draw our forces out of the town and secure it themselves," added Liu.

"Not likely."

"Come on, Viktor, you clearly know more than you're letting on, so spit it out."

They both waited for him to answer, and he took his time, taking another puff and blowing it out calmly.

"Volkov only keeps a small troop around him at any time. He calls on the few militia stationed nearby when he has to, but if trouble really strikes, he has to ask for help from larger Alliance worlds."

"And you know this, how?"

"I know because I know, like I know lots of things. Like you used to be a cop."

"That's really fucking observant," replied Liu.

"All right!" yelled Mason. "How many fighters does he have right now, and what do you think we can expect?"

"Maybe fifty that he will have called in. The other towns can't afford to give up any more than that. He won't want to call on the Alliance because then he'd have to explain this mess. So he'll bring in hired guns. That'll take a couple of days."

"We could strike now?" asked Liu.

"Long as you don't mind letting your pilot go."

"Why?" Mason asked.

"'Cos the Sheriff's department will have him off world

by morning. That's how they work."

Mason shook his head. He was now torn between the two options.

"As I said, Volkov needed to buy some time."

Mason looked to Liu for answers. He looked as suspicious of Viktor as he had done the first time.

"He could be right."

Liu tilted his head as if to ask, 'really?'

"Take it or leave it. Drag your heels and your buddy is gone."

"He's part of your crew too," stated Mason.

"Yeah, well I ain't ever met him."

Mason stepped up to Viktor and hauled him off to one side, though he only just moved due to his bulk. Mason leaned in to whisper.

"You signed up to this crew, so did Mitchell. We have a responsibility towards each other. You were a soldier, you must understand that?"

Viktor shook his head and sighed.

"You said you never fought in the war, and I can see it plain. If you had, you'd know how much bullshit that comment is. The war was every man for himself. There were as many enemies at my back as there were in front, and cowards and aplenty."

"I'm sorry to hear that."

"I don't want your sympathy. Just don't expect me to care about people like they were my brothers."

Mason could see there was no convincing him.

"Well, if you won't care, will you at least help?"

"It was already offered. It's what I'm being paid for, isn't it?"

"Yes."

They stepped back to Liu. He could see Liu hated everything Viktor was, but like Mason, he accepted the thug as a necessary element of their job.

"Right, let's start this again. I want Mitchell back in one piece, so how do we go about it?"

They went silent.

"Don't look at me. I don't know this planet any better than you," Liu said.

The silence was broken by shouts coming from outside. They rushed to the door and saw a column of three vehicles coming down the street. Armed gunmen were on top of the fore and aft vehicles. They were all heavy wheeled and with substantial armour, but the middle one was completely enclosed in mirrored glass.

"Liu, get to the roof."

He stepped to the middle of the room.

"Looks like Volkov is incoming! Three vehicles coming from the east. Everyone to their positions!"

"Where'd you want me?" Andrews asked from the table he was lying on. He was trying to get up, but Erin held him down.

"Get yourself to the kitchen and watch the back door.

Erin you stay with him."

She wasn't sure if they were being put into play or being sent to safety, and that made her uneasy, but she accepted anyway. Mason rushed back to the entrance and grabbed his rifle from the chair it rested on. He'd given his favourite rifle to Erin, as she'd grown attached to it. He was using a newer variant that he'd never got on with quite so well, but he always preferred pistols anyway.

The three trucks pulled up outside the bar in the middle of the road and drew to a halt. It was a clear sign that whoever was inside had information on their positions, and that made him uncomfortable. Gunmen leapt from the trucks, but they stood out front of the trucks without any attempt to search for cover, though machine gunners atop the two trucks were protecting them.

Mason was hunkered down at the doorway, only revealing enough of himself to see what was going on.

"What are they doing?" Viktor asked.

He was standing the other side of the doorway with a high calibre carbine.

"Where the hell did you get that?"

"You think I wear this long coat for fashion?"

"I just figured it was part of your whole badass image."

"Thanks," he replied, taking it as a compliment.

They watched the driver step out from the middle vehicle and open the door behind him, for what they could only imagine would be Volkov himself. The first thing they saw were boots with raised silver-plated heels hitting the ground. Then they saw him for the first time. He was of average height, though the boots lifted him a little. He wore a three-quarter length tan lightweight but formal coat. Over it was a dark green sash; he had a peaked cap of matching colour. It was a spectacle clearly intended to intimidate.

He was clean-shaven with a pipe in his mouth, which he smoked casually as if he had no care in the world. There was no obvious sign of a weapon on him, an arrogant and confident move in itself. His trousers were pressed with perfect lines, something rarely seen on a frontier world. His tie was the matching green pigment of his sash and cap, the same as worn by the local militia, and the official colour of the Alliance.

Volkov took a few paces towards the bar, stopped in the middle of the road, and stood defiantly smoking his pipe.

"Let's put a bullet in him now," whispered Viktor, raising his rifle to take the shot.

"No!" Mason ordered him.

"What the hell? He's right there. We could end this here and now."

"We aren't ready. We start a fight here, and it'll be a bloodbath, and where does that leave Mitchell?"

"Fuck Mitchell. He's one guy."

"And if it were you taken, instead of him?"

"I'd expect to get myself out of that shit."

"I'll call you to that when it happens."

"No chance," he replied with a grin.

Volkov finally spoke. His voice was confident and strong, and carried across the street and to the surrounding buildings.

"I am Colonel Michael Volkov! Am I speaking to Captain Mason?"

Mason lowered his weapon and stood up to join him.

"He'll gun you down."

"They shoot me, Viktor, you have my permission to riddle the bastard with everything you've got."

"I can hope."

I'm concerned. Viktor's a wild card and will provoke a fight for just the enjoyment fighting brings him.

"All of our lives are on the line here. Don't do anything stupid."

"Don't call me stupid."

Viktor seemed to take surprised offence at the term and looked as if he were awaiting an apology.

"Just don't get me killed, all right?" Mason asked.

"I can do that."

Mason propped his rifle at the side of the door and strode out empty handed, but in a relaxed manner with his hands at his waist and his trigger hand just centimetres from his handgun.

"Captain Mason, I presume?"

"That's me."

"Ah, the man I have been hearing so much about," he gestured back towards Hunter, standing at the vehicles with a rifle. He gave a scornful look.

"Haven't heard much about you, only the lackeys who do your work, badly I might add."

He smiled in response.

"Let me be absolutely clear. This is my town, my world. Whatever deal you have made with the people of this town is null and void, unless authorised by myself."

"These people are civilians. They aren't under your command. How they spend their money is their business."

"Yes, up to a point. But as the elected representative, I have a responsibility to uphold the law and quell any and all uprisings."

"Elected? I think some folk here might have something to say about that."

"You know elections are always about picking the right man for the job." He pointed to himself, "I'm the right man for the job."

Mason shook his head. He knew there was no point in pushing it.

"Now, I have a simple proposition for you. Return to your ship, where you can leave with no further consequences. Or, be charged with four counts of murder, and several more of assault. You will spend thirty years in prison unless you are killed during capture. Your crew will suffer a similar fate, except for that pretty girl I hear so much about, and your ship will be sold for scrap."

Mason was silent as he studied the man. He was growing angrier by the second, but his chief fear was that Viktor would be tipped over the edge and start shooting.

"Well, what'll it be, Captain?"

"Colonel, that's a real good offer there, but you see; ship's broken, and my pilot's missing. Till that's resolved, I ain't going anywhere, and seeing as that is the case, I intend to make some money while I'm on this world."

Volkov's calm smile turned to a frown. Mason could see he had grown used to getting everything he wanted, and it pleased him to see the discomfort he was bringing the bullying Colonel.

"I could have you shot dead where you stand," he spat.

Mason rose up proud and defiantly to stand tall.

"Likewise. One of my guys in there, he'd happily kill you even if it meant my death. Your men fire a single shot, and you won't live long enough to hear a second."

"What do you think this place is? Some circus where you can come in and make a handful of credits, and leave as you please?"

He looked past Mason to address the people of the town. Some were watching from windows in the shops and rooms above, but he knew many more were hunkered down in hearing distance as well.

"You made a big mistake hiring these guns! If you carry

on down this path, I promise you will regret it. I have never used violence against the people of this town, but if you persist, I will have no choice. You will suffer death, imprisonment, and the loss of your loved ones!"

He turned to walk away but stopped after a few paces and looked back.

"Don't die for a cause that doesn't exist, Captain."

Mason didn't respond but only waited for him to leave. Volkov sighed. He hadn't got the response he wanted.

"I'll tell you what. You have twenty-four hours grace to think this over. I give you my word that we will not enter this town again in that time. But when I do, and find you are still here, I will kill you. Do you and your friends a favour, get out while you can."

"Good day, Colonel," he replied.

Volkov climbed aboard, and Mason's attention turned to Hunter. The Sergeant was now armoured up and ready for war, and he had wide crazy eyes that wanted to murder Mason, there and then.

"Listen to the Colonel, Captain," he said. "You don't want another beating, because next time you won't survive it."

He spit on the ground and climbed aboard one of the trucks. The column turned and left. Viktor stepped up to his side, still clutching his rifle.

"Should have let me shoot him."

"You know I couldn't."

"I really don't."

Mason lifted up his comms unit. "All clear, gather up, we got some thinking to do."

A couple of minutes later they were once again at the table in Kaper's bar. It seemed to have become their new home.

"Really think he'll give us twenty-four hours?"

"Yes, I do, Ben."

"Why?"

"Because he wants to avoid a fight as much as the next person, Erin."

"Yeah, right," Viktor grumbled.

"Hey, you might fight for fun, but we do it for money."

"Your loss, Hughes."

"The Captain is onto something. Volkov is trying to muscle us out without a fight. He's done his best to intimidate us, now he'll want us to sleep and sweat on it. He's giving us as much time as possible to bug out."

"You'd like that, wouldn't you?" asked Viktor. "Just what you yellow VASI boys always want to do."

Hughes launched himself across the table and swung a punch at Viktor. His head snapped aside from the impact, but he quickly recovered and hauled Hughes over the table, throwing him across the room into a couple of chairs.

"This is no good," Liu said.

Mason leapt between the two of them, but Viktor threw him aside, grabbing his holster from his side. Just as his

NICK S. THOMAS

pistol got level to fire, a glass thrown by Hella with precise accuracy hit his gun hand. It smashed over the hand and gun, forcing him to release his grip. The fragments cut dozens of surface scratches into his skin. He quickly turned to face off against Hughes when he felt the barrel of a gun touch the side of his head.

"Sit down!" Mason shouted.

Viktor turned around, smiled at the Captain, and slowly reached down and picking up his pistol, holstering it carefully and taking his seat.

"How the hell can we expect to beat this bastard if we're fight each other?"

"We wouldn't have to if you'd let me take that shot on Volkov."

"There's more than one life we have to be worried about," replied Mason, as he holstered his pistol.

"We have limited time and two things on the agenda. One we have to get Mitchell back. Two, we have to get this town ready for the battle it faces."

"And if those two things aren't mutually exclusive?"

"We'll find a away, Hell. Viktor, you say Volkov is buying some time to get support here. Good, let's take that opportunity to do the work we need to."

"Or we could use it to go and blow his head off."

"No. We're on familiar terrain here, and I will not leave Mitchell to that fate. Where is he likely to be held?"

Kaper stepped up ready to answer, awaiting permission

to do so.

"Spit it out," Mason snapped.

"The Sheriff's department has a holding facility about a hundred kilometres west of here. It's where all dangerous prisoners are taken."

"Dangerous?" asked Andrews.

"I meant..."

"We know what you meant, thanks."

"We're gonna conduct a rescue operation amongst all of this?"

"If it were you facing the sentence he is, Hughes, would you want us to try?" asked Mason.

They all went silent as they thought about his situation.

"Here's what's gonna happen. We've already seen the Sheriff and his deputies aren't up to much, so I should be able to manage this with minimal help."

"I'm in," said Hella.

He was surprised to hear anyone volunteer so quickly.

"I've spent enough time behind bars to not wish it on anyone."

It was a surprising comment coming from someone so young, but he didn't have the time or luxury to pursue the matter.

"You volunteer, you get the job," he replied.

"I'll go," said Liu.

"No, you're in charge while I'm gone. Hughes, it's your time to step up. Liu, you'll be down on numbers, so just protect what we got. When we get back, we'll start on the defences."

"We can do it."

"No, Liu, we may think the bastard is holding off, but we don't know. I want you all on watch until the moment we get back."

"And if they attack while you're gone?"

"Well then at least you won't be caught with your pants down."

They all said nothing; knowing there was no point arguing. Mason gestured for Liu to go outside with him. As soon as they did, Liu was at him.

"You're leaving me with that animal?"

He knew Liu was referring to Viktor.

"Have to. I need one of us in each place to keep charge. He might be an animal, but he's our animal. Control him like one, and I have no doubt he will more than prove his worth."

"I don't like it."

"You don't have to like it. You just have to live through it."

They looked out, and the streets were now deserted. Shops were locked up, and nobody wanted to be seen in the open. There was a grim feeling in the air that they would come under attack at any moment.

"Sure you can get Mitchell out with the three of you?"

"I figure I can."

"In this daylight? Not much of a chance for any stealth."

"No, then we're gonna have to use a different approach."

"Shoot your way in? Not like we have the vehicles to do it."

"Not what I meant."

He leant around the door and shouted to Kaper.

"Get Avery to send his truck over here and his driver, ASAP!"

"Shall I tell him what for?"

"Just get him here!"

Liu knew already what he was planning.

"Not a bad idea, but once you're there, you still aren't packing a whole lot of firepower."

"Enough of your negative waves, this is gonna work. Get to your positions, and be ready for anything."

Liu passed him by and headed for the roof.

"We leave as soon as our ride gets here, should be no more than fifteen minutes!" He looked over at Hella. She still carried no gun of any kind. He paced over to the table of guns they'd collected from the militia they had killed and passed one up to her, but she refused to take it."

"Guns are a dirty business."

"Well we certainly aren't in the laundry cleaning one."

"You show me a situation where I would have needed one, and I'll happily comply."

She took a seat as they awaited the truck.

"Kaper, three sodas!" Mason called out.

He sat down and threw his feet up on the table in front of him. He noticed Hughes was sitting in his lightweight wheelchair. He'd powered his exo-skeleton down to preserve the energy for when they really needed it. He never asked how he lost the control of his legs, but it hardly seemed worth asking a man who was clearly a soldier who had seen more than a few battles. He turned to Hella. She still fascinated him.

"So, we haven't had much time to chat since you joined us."

"Not much to say."

"But you surely have a lot to tell. You must still be a teenager, but you fight with expert training. Stealth, close combat skills, knife fighting, and you trained on Melian."

"Melian?" Hughes asked.

From his reaction, the former soldier knew of the planet and what went on there as well. Viktor picked up on it and listened in.

"All those skills and no interest in firearms. If I had to guess, I'd say you were trained as an assassin, but at your age?"

"Girl's got to have her secrets."

"Really?" Hughes was now more interested.

"Never heard of Melian, that over VASI side."

"Yeah..it is," Hughes replied sternly. He took pleasure in Viktor's ignorance in the matter.

"So?"

"Why'd you want my history, Hughes? I don't know yours, or any of you."

"Career soldier, fought through the war, got hurt, medically discharged, and here I am."

"Don't go writing your life story anytime soon."

"Why?"

"Because you won't even fill a page."

Viktor laughed at his expense, and Mason couldn't help but find it funny. Hughes sat back and gave up, but it was Mason's turn.

"You this broody and dark by nature, or did you train for it?"

She could see he was trying to hook her in.

"All right, I'll bite. I was trained to kill, got pretty good at it."

"Right," Viktor replied sarcastically.

She kicked back her chair and approached him slowly but confidently. He turned and took a step until his back was against the doorframe. He didn't know how to respond to her. She passed within his personal space until her body lay against his.

"You're pretty handsome for a soldier, tall too," she whispered seductively.

He smiled a little and couldn't believe his luck. The others were fixated on her actions.

"That's quite a gun you wear, can I see it?" she asked.

"Uhh… yeah," he stammered.

He reached down to grip the pistol but found an empty holster. He looked down and saw it had gone. His eyes shot back to Hella. He froze as he felt her blade on his throat. Mason clapped as Viktor was still frozen, and for a second believed she might actually be willing to use the blade. Finally, she stepped back and handed him his Griswold. She sheathed the blade and went to sit back down. Viktor held his pistol in his hands and looked amazed.

"You know what they say about letting women near your money," joked Hughes.

"Impressive," Mason smiled.

"Oh...come on. Any pretty girl could do that, but would they if they knew I would fight back, no way! That rich kid could have done the same until you put it to the test against an opponent who wants to kill you."

"You're a bad loser."

"Hell, yeah, I am, Captain. Just never lost before to know."

The rest of them laughed.

"Okay, so maybe you are trained as what, an assassin? Or maybe you're just a streetwise kid who's learnt to get tough or else die," said Mason.

"Maybe, you make up your own mind."

Mason turned to Hughes who was still curious.

"You ever hear about VASI training up teenagers for this? Whatever this is. Espionage, sabotage, assassin, whatever."

"Few rumours maybe, but you can't believe a lot of that in the Army."

"Figures VASI would have girls do their fighting for them. That's about the first sensible thing I've heard all day," Viktor said.

The room went quiet as they all thought about the possibility of what she could be. It was both shocking and intriguing to all of them. Erin had never seen or met anyone like her.

"Could you teach me?" she asked. "To use a knife like you do?"

"Why?"

"Knife fighting is rough work, men's work."

"Apparently not, Viktor," said Erin.

Viktor grumbled and went quiet. It didn't sit well with him that he had been humiliated in front of them all.

"You know all this is fine and dandy, but in a real fight, you learn to hit hard and take a few punches. You'll live long and strong, like me."

Erin shook her head.

"If I ever want to live a life of hard drinking, fist fights, and whores, maybe I'll come and ask you for advice."

"Wow," Mason muttered.

"Hey, ain't such a bad life," Viktor smiled.

She recoiled in disgust. She knew he wasn't joking.

"I'll teach you to use a knife, but I don't work for free, Erin. I heard you can shoot."

"Better than most I've ever seen," Mason joined in.

"Teach me to shoot like that, and I'll teach you to use a blade."

"You're on."

"Well isn't this a merry fucking day," Viktor sneered.

They all chose to ignore the brash comment.

"All that specialist training and you never learnt to shoot?"

"Lot of things to a job, Captain. You can shoot, but can you fly?"

"Yes, just not very well."

"Same here, but with guns."

"You know how to fly?" asked Viktor sceptically.

"I do," she quickly retorted.

He looked sheepish and turned away to look out to the street.

"Guess that told you, Max," Liu said.

"You could really fly the Lady?" he asked.

"I can. I just wouldn't want to. Flying isn't my thing."

"Your truck's incoming!" yelled Viktor.

Mason got up and rushed to the door and checked with his own eyes. It was indeed Ryant's well-worn heavy haulage truck that had delivered their components, in what now felt like an age ago.

"Hella, Hughes, haul ass!"

They got up to join him, but he could see Liu was still not happy with the situation.

"If they come at us in the next couple of hours, we're probably fucked," he whispered.

"Can you never see the positive in any situation?"

"I can imagine ten million credits, Max, but I'm having a hard time working out how we'll ever see it."

"You just hold down the fort. Make sure Vik doesn't do anything stupid."

The truck ground to a halt, and Avery climbed out.

"Where's Cayne?"

"Locked up safe, same as most of the town. I'll drive you wherever you want to go. Hell, I ain't doing any business till this is all figured out."

"All right, I want you to take us to the Sheriff's lockup where they take prisoners. I need you to fake a breakdown, a hundred metres from their position, and then go ask them for help. Once you and them get back to the truck, we'll take it from there. Think you can do that?"

"And if they don't care to come and help with the truck?"

"You tell them you're delivering some parts for Volkov for a friend of his. You think that'll work?"

"If they truly believe Volkov has ordered it, they will do all that I need."

"Then you better work on your acting skills."

"It'll take a bit over an hour to get there."

"Then let's move out."

He nodded for the other two to join him, went to

the back of the truck, and climbed in. There were a few component crates in the back, but it was mostly empty. There were no comforts whatsoever, except for the canopy which kept the sun and dust off.

"Pretty simple plan, think it'll work?"

"You just work your magic when they get to us, Hell, and we'll be in and out in no time."

CHAPTER TEN

They'd never gone west of the town before, but it didn't look any different to where the ship had come down. It was a coarse rocky terrain lacking in moisture. Despite that, the smooth suspension of the truck swallowed up most of the hard impacts along the way. It was a small team to be taking on a rescue mission, and they all knew it.

"Here's how we're gonna do this. They get near this truck, and we take them down silently. No need to kill them if you don't have to. We need at least one uniform clean for me to wear. I'll approach the office as one of theirs. Meantime, I want Hughes to be fifty paces behind me and ready for support when things kick off. Hella, find another way in through the roof, sides, anywhere you can."

"It's a prison. Ain't gonna be any."

"I'll find something, Hughes."

"We're passing them now!" yelled Avery.

They ducked down low into the truck be. Mason hugged the tailgate and stayed just high enough to get a view of the place as they trundled past. It was quiet. Three vehicles were parked up outside. It appeared the prison could hold only a dozen prisoners at the most. It was a small complex with an accommodation block for the staff next door. Nobody was visible from outside.

"Doesn't look too bad," he whispered.

The truck passed the Marshals' station without incident as they'd expected. At that point, Avery cut the power of the truck and let it roll to a halt. He jumped from the cab and walked around to the back to address them one last time.

"You sure about this now?"

"Yes, just one question. We start shooting, you gonna have a problem with people getting killed here?"

"As long as it ain't us. Those marshals are in Volkov's pocket. They've never lifted a finger to help us."

"Good to know."

Mason went to crawl to the back and through the hatch into the cab.

"Wait till they pass."

Half an hour had gone by, and they were all getting concerned. They were worried Avery had turned them in, and it was becoming all too apparent that if it were the case, they were in a giant coffin.

"Come on," whispered Mason.

"We can't stay here any longer. We'll just have to go in."

"No, Hughes, let's give him a chance. They're probably just dragging their heels."

"And if they're waiting for Volkov to arrive and blow the shit out of us?"

"Well then none of it matters, does it?"

"All the work you do this messy?"

"We usually we have a solid plan. Can't say it always goes the way we want it."

Hughes shook his head.

"Look, he's still alive," Hella said. "Must be doing something right."

"Yes, they're coming," said Hughes.

It wasn't long before they could hear the footsteps; and their previous concerns replaced by new ones. The plan was coming together, but timing was now everything. They could hear the discussion Avery was having with the two deputies.

"I still can't believe you didn't keep your truck maintained, you, the parts guy."

"I deal in ship parts. I ain't no auto mechanic."

"And there I was thinking there was more to a job than one thing. Volkov will have your balls for this."

"And yours too if he knew you left me here."

Three sets of footsteps passed them, heading towards the engine bay of the vehicle. Hughes noticed out of the corner of his eye that Hella was already on the tailgate of the vehicle. She flipped herself nimbly up onto the top of the canvas roof with barely a single sound. It was a sight unnatural to him that sent a quiver down his spine. She moved more like a stalking cat than a human.

Mason sat in the driver's cab and could see them approaching along the vehicle's side. Avery had kept them close to the truck just as he had wanted. They were completely unaware of the danger they were walking into. He pushed the door open hard. It smashed into the first deputy and launched him off his feet.

Before he had even landed, Hella was airborne and descending on the other man. He was forced down onto his back with the weight of her body, and she drove a quick punch into his head. It knocked him unconscious against the hard ground. Mason was quickly out of the truck and stormed towards his opponent who was fumbling to get his pistol out. He slammed his boot down on the man's inner elbow, and he squirmed in pain. He pulled out his own pistol, flipped it to grip by the barrel, and cracked it down on his head. Blood burst from the man's head, but he managed to lash out and push Mason aside. The deputy was stunned and again tried to reach for his pistol. Mason rushed to his back, taking him into an arm lock and pulling him to the ground. He wrapped his leg over the man's gun hand until he passed out from the hold on his neck.

Mason sighed in relief, "That was close."

Hella grabbed his hand and hauled him to his feet, but only just. She felt half his weight and probably was.

"What the hell's going on here?" came a call.

They both turned around in a panic, and Mason's heart stopped when he saw a third deputy draw out his pistol fifteen metres back from the truck. The crack of a laser weapon rang out and hit him in the chest. He was dead on his feet and slumped down to the ground. Hughes jumped from the back of the vehicle with his rifle in hand. Mason wanted to thank him, but they had more pressing concerns.

"This is gonna get ugly quick!" he yelled, rushing to the back of the truck. He grabbed his rifle and rushed towards the building.

"What do you want me to do?" Hella asked, as they made a break for the office front.

"Same as before. Find a way in and get to Mitchell!"

A uniformed militiaman appeared at the door with a rifle but was riddled with a double tap from both of them.

"Christ, ain't this supposed to be a Marshal's department?" Hughes asked.

"Volkov must have sent some help. At least that's taken away some of his number from the town!"

"What a relief."

They got to the door the man had come from and burst through inside as quickly as they could. They found the counter empty, but voices further into the complex could be heard. For a moment they thought they had gotten away with it, until a loud siren sounded off.

"Shit, we gotta move."

They rushed behind the desk and down the only corridor that continued past it. Two militiamen rushed towards them but hadn't got their weapons raised. Mason fired two shots into each of them, continued moving, and knocked them both down. Another rushed out from a side door, slamming Hughes into the wall opposite. Mason turned in time to see Hughes drive a knee into the man. It hit like a train, causing what must have been major internal injuries. It dropped him to the floor.

"Those legs do more than walk then?"

Hughes smiled. "They aren't all bad."

They rushed past several cells; the prisoners watching in shock as the two gunmen passed them.

"That's him!" Mason shouted.

Mitchell was flat out on a slab of concrete resembling a bed, but with none of the niceties. He was conscious but barely lucid. He hadn't even noticed their presence.

"Felix! Can you hear me?"

He turned slowly and smiled. "Boss?"

It was the only occasion when he wouldn't rib him for saying it.

"Can you walk?"

"Uhhh...walk? Why would I want to walk, Boss? I want to sleep."

"He's out of it," whispered Hughes.

"They must have pumped him full of drugs, a guarantee that he goes down for good."

"I hear he's a junkie. Maybe he got himself into this."

"No, not a chance. He's come through for us, and we're gonna get him out of this."

Mason stepped back and fired at the locking blade. It sheared off. He hauled the cage door open and rushed inside.

"Mitchell, don't you worry, we're gonna get you out of here. You're gonna be all right."

Christ, Felix, we really are in the shit here, he thought.

He could see Hughes was thinking the same.

"Where's Hella?" he asked.

Mason looked around, but there was no movement, except for the other prisoners. Glass smashed down beside them, and a body of a militiaman dropped from the roof, hitting the floor beside them.

"Christ!" Hughes shouted.

They looked up and Hella dropped in through the skylight she had clearly just thrown a man through. She landed down beside him as softly as she could.

"They were waiting for us."

"How many, Hell?"

There's another three up there like him."

"On your tail?" Hughes asked.

"Dead," she replied.

It wouldn't have been believable, had they not seen her handy work the last few days. With the skylight gone through, they could hear the shouts of troops gathering outside.

"How many more you think are out there?"

"More than we can handle."

"Volkov must have really pulled out the stops."

"He must have known I'd come. He's betting on capturing me will put an end to his troubles."

"Smart."

"Maybe, but he just fucked with the wrong guy."

A megaphone cut in and echoed around the room.

"You are surrounded. Lay down your weapons, and come out with your hands up!"

"I didn't take this job to go to prison."

"Nobody's going to prison, Hughes. Have a little faith. Let's look at our options. This place got an internal garage?"

"I'm on it," Hella said, and she rushed off to scout the building.

Mitchell was rambling and sitting down against some of the bars of his cell. Mason knelt down beside him and slapped him in the face.

"Come on, Felix. You gotta hold it together!"

"Boss, let me sleep."

Mason pulled a medipack out of a pouch on his vest and took out an e-shot.

"All the stuff in his body, you sure you want to do that? It could kill him."

"We don't get him on his feet in the next two minutes, and he's dead anyway. Way I figure it Mitchell's body has survived every substance known to man. If anyone can manage it, it's him."

"Not exactly something you'd want to be noted for."

"Better than being dead."

He held the device onto Mitchell's throat and clicked the button on the top. Mitchell's eyes immediately opened wide, and he shot to life. He stared deep into Mason's eyes and for a moment wasn't sure of his surroundings.

"Where the hell are we?"

"Where do you think?"

He looked around at the bars and the other prisoners.

"Ah, shit. I feel like hell."

Hella ran back into the room. "They've got four ducted fan bikes in the garage."

"They could have left those for us. No protection whatsoever, so they could gun us down no problem."

"You underestimate us," replied Mason.

He got up and rushed to the other cells to address the prisoners.

"I'm gonna give you all a chance to get out of here. There are bikes waiting for you. You want out?"

They erupted in excitement, for he knew they were all resigned to a similar fate Mitchell had been. He had no idea if they deserved to be there or not, but he didn't have the luxury of caring. He pulled out a smoke grenade from his belt and handed it to Hughes.

"You wait with them at the door. Do not let them out until I say. Then pop both the smokes and let 'em go."

"But, how?"

"Just do it. Once the doors are open, you head for the roof immediately."

"How?"

"There's a ladder in the garage," Hella said.

"Right, you grab that, and get it set up to that skylight." He lifted his comms unit. "Avery, you there?"

It was silent for a few seconds until he responded with a whisper.

"What the hell is going on, Mason?"

"We need a way out..."

"Ain't no way I can get through those boys."

"Just listen. We're gonna pop some smoke grenades in a second. You wait ten seconds and then come for us. Get as close to the east wall as you can. Avoid the entrance. We're gonna blow it."

"How you getting to the truck?"

"Off the roof."

"What?"

"No choice, please just do it. Remember, ten seconds after you see the smoke, get up to the east side wall."

"Yeah...all right," he replied hesitantly. "Good luck."

"And to you."

Mason pulled out a C11 charge from his webbing. Besides a little ammunition, it was all the gear he had left at his disposal. He went towards the entrance and hunkered down so as not be seen over the desk when he reached it.

This is gonna be damn close!

He put the charge on the desk and noticed a glimmer of movement above it. It was a shadow from troops right outside the door. He knew they were close to breaching. He pulled out his pistol.

"Stay back!" he yelled, firing random shots in quick succession out towards the door. He flicked the arming switch on the explosive and rushed back, firing a few more shots.

"We're running out of time!" he shouted.

Hella was propping up the ladder as he arrived.

"Hughes, you ready?" he asked over the comms.

"Ready."

"Do it."

They heard the faint whine of the mechanical doors of the garage lifting.

"Throwing smoke."

A few seconds later they heard the ducted fans of the bikes spin up. Mason began to count the ten seconds in his head.

Ten, nine.

"Get up there," he said to Hella.

She didn't hesitate. She almost ran up the ladder at a surprising speed. Hughes rushed out towards him and scrambled up after her.

Eight, seven, six.

He looked up. Hughes had made it to the roof. He lifted up the trigger for the device, praying it wouldn't bring the building down on them. His thumb tapped the trigger, and an ear splitting blast soared through the structure, rocking the ground beneath them. Dust filled the air, and Mason took his chance to get up to the roof. They heard a hail of gunshots as the militia fired at the bikes, but the other prisoners were not their concern.

A second crashing sound could be heard below, and Hughes looked over the edge to see Avery's truck smashing through two copters which had been brought in for cover my the militia. The rotors at a corner of each were smashed apart as the hulking vehicles were brushed aside.

"That's Avery. He's coming all right!" he shouted to Mason.

The Captain got to the rooftop and rushed to the edge, but Avery's truck came in too close and smashed into the structure, causing it to shake and almost take them off their feet.

"Onto the roof!" Mason ordered.

He climbed onto the ledge and fired two shots into the canvas before leaping and hoping for the best. Hella and

Hughes were close behind, and all three crashed through the canvas, landing hard in the cargo bay with no finesse at all.

"Go!" Mason screamed.

The truck pulled away as fragments of the wall it had crashed into collapsed down behind them. Hughes was the first up and lifted his rifle to fire some covering shots, but laser pulses flew at them. One clipped part of his exoskeleton, and he twisted violently and dropped down below the tailgate. Mason rushed to fill his place. There was no time for checking on him as they made a break for it.

He took a few shots, but Avery turned quickly and put the prison building between them and most of the shooters. They were gaining speed and were quickly out of range. He turned back. Hughes was trying to pull himself up onto the raised side runners of the bed. Hella was sitting back and dusting off her coat, ignoring him completely. It was the first realisation for Mason that she really was what had been suspected.

She shows no emotion or empathy at all.

Mason reached down and hauled him up into a seated position.

'You all right?"

He looked down at the wound. His trousers and skin beneath had been clipped badly below the knee.

"I can't feel that far down, anyway."

Mason looked back up at his face to see he was telling the truth, but the exoskeleton support was also snapped beside the wound.

"I ain't gonna be walking anytime soon."

A laser rushed past the side of the truck as he said it.

"Can you still shoot?"

Mason reached down, took a hold of his rifle, and threw it into the soldier's hands. They could see two copters approaching rapidly. They were far faster and more nimble than the hulking vehicle they were making their getaway in. Mason fired quickly; the shot knocked one of the militia off the lead vehicle. Hughes joined in, but Mason looked back to Hella. She was still sitting calmly behind him. He pulled his pistol and tried to give it to her. She refused.

"Until I can use it to perfection, I'm not using it at all."

"We ain't got time for your bullshit. Take the damn gun!"

She snatched it from his hands and moved up between the two of them.

"Shoot something!" he yelled.

She loosed off a shot, but it went far wide of its target.

"Shit, you really can't shoot."

"Screw you!" she shouted as she tried harder.

One of the copters zoomed past into their blind spot.

"This one's mine!"

She flipped out onto the rooftop as she had done before and quickly leapt onto the vehicle that was coming up beside them. She was out of the other two's view, so they turned their attention on the other vehicle.

"Take their fans out!" Mason yelled.

They both focused their fire on the front fans of the quadcopter, and within seconds smoke was pouring from them, and the vehicle shut down. Mason took a hold of the rear of the roof and jumped onto the tailgate to check on Hella. She was at the controls of the vehicle. The two occupants were dead. He smiled back in response and sat back down opposite Hughes.

"She okay?"

"More than okay. Maybe she can't shoot for shit, but God help any of us if we end up in a knife fight with her."

They eventually rolled back into town to cautious looks from the few who were out to see them, and the many others who watched from their windows. Liu was waiting in the porch of the bar and looked in disbelief. He hadn't expected Mason to return any other way except battered.

Avery stopped the truck outside the Digger to a cheer of applause from the crew who came out to join Liu. Mason leapt off the back and helped Hughes down. He could only stand on one leg while Mason helped him hobble along. Erin was quick out the door to assist his other side as Hella rode the copter up and parked behind them. The bodies were still sitting in the seats behind her. It was an uncomfortable sight to behold.

"You get him?" asked Liu. Mitchell stumbled and fell

out the back of the truck.

"Yeah, but he's a mess."

"No more than you," snapped Mitchell from his position in the dirt.

"Avery! Damn fine job you did out there!"

He turned to the others. "Saved our lives."

"Avery!"

There was no response.

Liu stepped up beside the cab of the vehicle. His face turned to stone. He pulled the door open and reached inside. He looked back at the others with sad eyes.

"He's dead," he said solemnly.

Mason handed Hughes over to Kaper who had come to greet them and stepped up to the cab himself. A laser shot had struck him through the cab and inflicted a mortal wound on his torso.

"He held on till he got you back safe," said Liu.

"A brave man."

"Yes, but no less dead."

The two of them stepped down from the truck. Viktor stood at the door of the bar with his arms crossed and looking moody.

"Great job, brought one man back at the loss of another. Great work."

"Not now, Vik," Mason sighed.

"I never knew you cared about these folk."

"I don't, Liu, but I'd like to think I wasn't working for a

man who'd risk a load of our lives for one."

"Have you no soul?" asked Erin.

Viktor smiled back. "I'm in this life for number one, me. I'll fight for money, but not some misplaced sense of loyalty."

"That why you were kicked out of the Alliance Army?" Hughes asked.

Viktor strode up to the wounded ex-soldier still being held up by Kaper and Erin. He smiled for a second, and then quickly punched Hughes in the face. He dropped from their grip and almost hit the ground.

"Viktor!"

He snapped around, glaring at the Captain. Mason could feel trouble brewing, and he knew it was time to have it out while they still had the luxury of doing so.

"We're in this together, Vik. We all agreed it, so let's start acting like professionals."

"Exactly my point," he replied. "Ever since we got this job, you have failed at every opportunity to seal the deal and get paid. I could have killed Volkov with one shot. One shot! One, bang, down. Instant pay cheque. Thank you, ladies and gentlemen, move on, next job. But no, you had to protect everyone and let him go, and where are we now? One man dead and one a fucking wreck."

"You want to leave this crew, you're welcome to anytime, but while you're here, you follow my orders whether you like it or not!"

Hughes was helped back to his feet and spat out blood on the floor. It partly spread over onto Viktor's boots. He looked down in disgust, and his hand grew nearer to his pistol.

"Don't even think about it, Vik. Remember who the boss is here."

"The Boss? 'Cos that's a title and a job you ain't seemed happy about since I came on board. Looks like you aren't up to the job. Maybe you don't even want it. Maybe it's time someone more capable takes it on, huh?" he asked the group.

None of them seemed to give their approval, and Erin look on with absolute horror of what was even happening while she was supporting a wounded man; and a dead one lay in the vehicle beside them.

"So we are a team, and the best man should lead. Maybe it's my turn?" he asked.

Hella began to circle behind him, but he had already anticipated her move and turned, pointing his finger at her.

"Don't even think about it, you crazy bitch. Next time you touch me will be your last."

She held up her hands as if to look innocent and took a few paces back.

"Didn't know you were so emotional about it," she replied.

Mason could see it was escalating and knew only he

could put an end to it.

"Viktor!"

The hulking man turned around to face off against him. He waited for Mason to speak and clenched his fists.

"All right, so you want a shot at being the Captain."

"Max?"

"No, no, Liu, if he wants a shot at me, he's welcome to take it."

"What the hell are we doing here? Fighting each other with the enemy on our doorstep?"

Ben Liu approached him so they could talk privately, but Mason interrupted him.

"We need him. I put him in his place, and he's the weapon we need him to be. We put him down now, and we're down a fighter worth more than his weight in credits."

"And if you can't beat him?"

Mason looked at him in surprise. "Your confidence is overwhelming."

"Just being realistic." He turned and looked at Vik's intimidating presence.

"I want this cleared up before the real fight begins. I want to know I can rely on everyone in the team when the time comes."

Ben shook his head. "I hope you're right."

"Okay, Vik," said Mason. "Here's the deal. No guns, no blades, no weapons of any kind. We fight it out here and now till one of us submits or can no longer fight."

"Sounds good."

"But let's be clear about this. If you win, you can step up to run this gig. If I win, you accept by command and start respecting my authority."

"It's a deal."

Erin was speechless. She let go of Hughes and stepped forward to intervene, but Hella grabbed her arm and stopped her.

"They need to do this."

"Why? What is there to prove?"

"Who calls the shots."

"A team divided is a team broken," Hughes explained.

"So, what? You want this?"

"Yeah, sure, just as long as the Captain wins."

None of them wanted to imagine the possibility of Viktor taking charge of the outfit. Vik pulled off his coat, revealing his strong physique. He looked like a man born naturally large and who'd worked with his body his entire life. He smiled as he unclipped his gun belt and dropped it down beside his coat. Mason could see he was looking forward to the fight. He threw off his own gear, and the two of them stepped out into the middle of the road.

Viktor stood a full head taller than Mason, and despite the Captain being well built himself, he looked like a boy compared to the towering ex Alliance soldier.

"We're gonna get this sorted and have the job done by

morning."

"Keep dreaming, Viktor."

Viktor lunged forward quickly with a right hook which was surprisingly swift, and Mason narrowly ducked under. He knew he couldn't afford to get tied up by the heavier fighter. He kicked to the inside of Vik's leg, but it barely wobbled him. Vik responded with a barrage of jabs and hooks, closing the distance. Mason fended them off, but Viktor was on top of him. He protected his head, but Vik dropped low and hit up with an uppercut that took the wind out of him.

The Captain was hunched over from the impact, and Viktor shoved him over onto the hard surface of the street.

"Come on, I haven't had my fun yet!" Viktor sneered.

Mason coughed and spluttered as he tried to refill his lungs with air.

"Is this the man you follow? You're paid to fight, and you want him leading you?"

Mason got to his feet and took up a stance to continue. Viktor came back at him with the same three combination, two jabs and a right hook. Mason voided to his left and hit him full on in the face, following it with a left, causing him to stumble back. He could see it was a shock to Viktor.

Vik came right back at Mason with a jab, and then quickly closed the distance and got into a standing clinch. He drove a knee up into Mason, further compounding his painful ribs, pushed between Mason's arm and head, driving an elbow down onto his neck.

The strike drove Mason down onto his knees and almost broke his collarbone. He quickly reacted by hitting Viktor in the groin with the hardest punch he could deliver, followed by a second and a third. Viktor howled in pain. Mason launched up with an uppercut to his jaw, sending him crashing to the ground like falling timber, but he wasn't finished. Mason stamped on his stomach and punched him in the face. Blood to burst from his nose.

Despite the punishment, Vik was still trying to get up. Mason offered out his hand to help him up. Viktor took it, as he knew he would. He hauled him up and twisted to his right side, driving his elbow into Vik's shoulder blade, still maintaining a grip on the arm and driving him face down into the ground. All of Mason's weight was on his back, and he held the arm back at the very limit before it would break in the socket. Viktor groaned but despite the pain, refused to go as far as screaming.

"Tap out, Vik, Tap out!"

He tried to fight it, but Mason only drove his elbow in deeper.

"All right, all right!"

"All right, what?" asked Mason.

"All right, you win."

"And?"

"And I accept you're the Boss."

"No, I'm the Captain. And what else?"

"And... I'll follow your orders."

"Well, all right then."

Mason released his grip, spun him over, and hauled him to his feet. Both were nursing wounds. Vik still had a smile on his face even though blood was dripping into his mouth, but it was now an amused grin. Mason could see he had won the man's respect.

"You fight dirty."

"Only as dirty as I have to, Vik," he replied, patting him on the back. Mason strolled back to the others triumphantly, but still holding his painful ribs.

"All that worth it?" asked Erin.

He stopped and replied sternly.

"Yes. Look at him. In a fight he's worth two or three of you, and now he's on our side."

CHAPTER ELEVEN

Mason lay in bed. The sun had hardly gone down, but he was nursing his wounds. He knew the medipads he was wearing would fix the worst of it overnight, but right then it still hurt like hell. His body hurt all over from a combination of everything that had happened that day. The lights were low, but he couldn't sleep. He heard footsteps approaching from the hallway, and a soft shadow was cast into the room. The footsteps were too light to be any of the men, and not light enough to be Hella.

"What can I do for you, Erin?"

She stepped through into the room and sat down on the edge of his bed.

"How are you feeling?"

"Peachy."

"What if you'd have lost?"

"But I didn't lose, did I? Think of losing and you will."

"Was it worth it?"

"Yes," he replied confidently. "Vik never wanted to run this outfit. He just wanted to know I was capable of doing so."

"And beating him into submission did that?"

Mason nodded in response. "I just guaranteed his loyalty for at least a good while, and that's a valuable thing."

"Is every mission you do this eventful?"

"They have their moments, but this one is certainly on the edge. We choose the jobs we take carefully, but hitting ground on this planet was not our choice. It was never an ideal situation or a perfect job to take from the beginning."

"So why did you take it?"

"Because the money was too good to say no, and with it in arm's reach, it was hard to say no."

"I thought..."

"What?"

"I thought maybe you were doing it for these people."

"Wealthy landowners who are too stupid to fight for what's theirs? Come on."

"I don't buy it. Nobody risks this much for money."

"Really? Go ask Hughes how he lost the use of his legs, and how much he got paid for the privilege."

Erin could see the good in Mason and wasn't willing to accept he was a mercenary first and foremost. Maybe he had started to feel a little for the town's people, but he still wouldn't have helped without the paycheque.

"How's Mitchell doing?" he asked.

"A mess. He's coming down from a major trip, and he's sweating buckets, but he'll live. That was impressive, you risking all to get one of the crew back. Would you do the same for any of us?"

"Yes."

"Why?"

"Because when I go into combat, I want to know that everyone on the team would do the same for me if it ever came to it."

"And that's what is most important to you, trust?"

"I guess so. In the end what we do is just a job. What matters is the team."

"So you're a family?"

Mason thought about it for a moment. "I guess so. Never really had one, and you?"

"What?"

"Family?"

"I barely knew them. They died when I was young. I was brought up on Mikula."

"You don't sound much like an orphan."

"My guardians were wealthy, is all."

"Were?"

"They aren't my guardians anymore."

"So you've parted ways with your old life?"

"Yes, I was heading to Veni before I got captured."

"Why?"

"Because I used to live there a long time ago, and I have business there."

"What kind of business?"

She looked away and refused to answer.

"Fine, you keep it to yourself. But if and when that business becomes profitable, and you want someone to work with you, you let me know."

She nodded in agreement, but Mason got the sense it wasn't a job that she meant. He opened his mouth to pry further, but she quickly retorted with a change of subject.

"All we've been through here, and we aren't any closer to doing what we were paid to do. Feels like we're slowly being ground down."

"I'll admit it hasn't gone too smoothly so far, but we've now got the whole team together. Volkov's ultimatum is fast approaching, and he can't walk away. He has to come at us or look foolish and weak."

"Maybe if people cared less about how they looked, and more about how they acted, we wouldn't be here."

"Yeah, well it's easy to say what could be in a perfect world. That all men and women could be equal, abolish poverty, and give everyone the good life. You should know your history. Veni tried exactly that, and look where it got them."

She couldn't argue with that.

"And when he does come, think we can stop him?"

"In all honesty, this ain't our kind of fight. This is a

grunt's fight. We plan our ops to hit the enemy hard when they are at their weakest, and get out before they can respond with all their force."

"But this time the enemy is bringing everything to bear."

"Yes, then I guess we'll find out just how good we are at soldiering."

He yawned wide, but Erin could tell he was faking. He wanted to be alone, but she didn't mind and knew he was really exhausted.

"I'll be on first watch. We'll take yours. You need all the hours you can get tonight."

"Thanks," he said, surprised.

She left him to it. For a moment he thought about the army preparing to roll over them, but exhaustion soon overcame him, and he faded into a deep sleep. He was awoken hours later to the sound of shots from the rooftop. He leapt out of bed, realising the sun was up, and he'd been out for a long while. He'd gone to bed dressed and with his boots on. Grabbing his rifle, he rushed to the roof.

"We've got company!" shouted Hughes who was on watch. He was propped up with a crutch under one arm, making up for the fact one of his legs wasn't working, but he still had his rifle slung across his front and ready to use. Mason arrived in time to see a small fast ship come in to land. Its wingspan was small enough it could come down in the street, and so clearly couldn't carry much of an attack force.

The ship was brand new and expensive, a lavish method of transport that few they ever met would use.

"Think it's Volkov?"

"I'd have said so, Hughes. Not many others who fly a thing like that."

But coming right into town without his army? Mason asked himself. *Something tells me this isn't Volkov at all.*

Hughes laid his crutch aside, leaned against the wall of the rooftop for support, and lifted his rifle up onto it ready to fire.

"I don't like this at all," he stated.

"Let's just be sure who's inside before we start shooting."

The engines powered down and a ramp lowered down into the street. Feet were the first thing they could see from the rooftop, as a lone person stepped out and into view. Mason's face turned from curiosity to a smile. He recognised the face.

"Hold your fire!"

Carter stepped into view from the ship. He was the last person Mason had expected to see. He rushed to the stairs, storming down them to get to the street to see the Boss. As he passed through the bar on the ground floor, he noticed Viktor sprawled out in a chair and barely awake. He looked like he had slept there all night.

"Friend of yours?" he asked.

"The old Boss."

"What's he doing here?"

"No idea."

Mason rushed out through the doors and saw Liu had already got out before him.

"I'm gone for a few days, and look at the shit you land yourself in."

"Wasn't really our choice. Foxy Lady was almost the end of us."

"You don't treat her right. She'll take everything you've got to give."

Mason was eyeing up the lavishly expensive little transport.

"And this amazing machine? In all the time I've known you, you never bought anything so flash."

"Well, when you get to retirement, and have a whole bundle of cash to spend, you realise it's time to start spending it when you're still about to enjoy it."

Mason patted him on the shoulder and led him towards the bar. Erin was approaching from the east where she had been stationed. Mason gestured for her to join them.

"Been recruiting?" Carter asked.

"Had too. We were down on numbers, and for this job we need shooters."

"And she's up to the task?"

"Better believe it, but she ain't the only girl I hired."

"Times are changing."

"Not really. You're just getting older."

Carter laughed, and they went inside.

"This is Viktor. Hughes was the guy on the roof who nearly took your head off."

"Good to know."

"So what are you doing here?"

"I came to warn you, Max. This job has been kicking around a few years for good reason. Nobody was stupid enough to accept it."

"But the money is great."

The Boss took him by the arm and led to him to a corner at the back of the room where they could talk privately. They took a seat, and Kaper was quick to lay down drinks on the table for them both. The Boss took his drink with suspicion.

"It ain't poisoned."

"That's not what I was worried about. They've got their hooks into you here."

"It's just a few drinks as a thank you while we work."

The Boss went quiet as he took a sip and at least enjoyed the taste.

"So why are you here? You said you wanted to warn me, but you didn't have to come in person to do that."

"Yes I did, because you're a stubborn son of a bitch. I don't care what they're offering. I didn't give this job a second look after learning some of the details. It ain't our kind of work."

"And whose kind of work is it?"

"Oh, I don't know, Max, and frankly, I don't care. We aren't humanitarians. We do this job for money and expect to a reasonably solid chance of surviving it."

"You don't do the job anymore. You retired."

He shook his head. "You know exactly what I mean. Hit and runs, assassinations, rescues, anything where we can use and exploit small numbers with careful planning. This is a stand up fight against an army."

"Then what do you suggest?"

"Give back any money you have taken, and get the hell out of here! Plenty of other work out there."

"How did you even know we were here, anyway?"

"You put out a call for operators."

"Still keeping an eye on the usual channels, then?"

"Always. Max, it's just not worth giving your life up for."

Mason sat back and thought about it for a moment. He wouldn't have given it any consideration coming from anyone else, but from the Boss it was cause for concern.

"You came here because you knew it'd be almost impossible to change my mind."

"Sure did."

"And what chance did you think you'd have?"

"Not a lot, but I wasn't gonna leave you here without a try. What is keeping you here? How is it worth it?"

The Boss could see Mason had changed in the few days they had been apart, and he himself was starting to feel it.

"So come on, spill it. This isn't all about the money, is it?"

Mason shook his head.

"You know all the shit jobs we've done. The people we've killed and the people we've worked for. That last mission we did together was the first one in a long time that actually felt good."

"Why?"

"Rescuing an innocent girl from a place like that. You tell me it didn't feel good?"

"But we were paid good money by the Gutierrez family to save her ass."

"No, not Skylar Gutierrez. Erin."

The Boss was taken aback. He looked back and could see her leaning at the entrance of the bar, looking out down the street with Mason's rifle slung on her shoulder.

"We didn't have to save her, and nobody else was coming for her. She's here because of us. Didn't that make you feel a little bit good? A little like our job was worth more than just the money we're paid?"

"It was nice we could help and all, but is it going to change the way I see the world? I dunno. You get soft in this job, and you get dead."

"Maybe, just maybe we can do the right thing, save some lives. Save some people from being robbed, and make a shit load of money in the process. As long as we make it through, what's not to like?" asked Mason.

"Well, you're the Boss now. It's your call."

"No, I'm the Captain, you're the Boss. And you came, so what will you do now?"

He took a deep breath, sipping his drink while he thought it over.

"You really are set about staying and seeing this through, aren't you?"

He nodded.

"Then what's one more gig? I'll stand with you."

"What happened to retirement?"

"Retirement is for sissies. It just took me a little while to figure that out."

"Not so long," he replied.

Mason was more than pleased to have the Boss along, but it also saddened him that Carter hadn't managed to break free from the work he had waited so long to get away from.

"You sure you want to do this?"

"Why not? Not got a whole lot else planned. But you're still in charge. I'm just here to help."

"Who's the old guy?" Hella asked.

They turned around. She was at the door.

"Why aren't you on watch?" asked Mason.

She lifted her hand and tapped her wrist. He looked down to see it was on the hour.

"Liu has taken over."

She turned her attention back to the Boss.

"You're a real charmer, aren't you?" he asked her.

"Made quite a statement landing that thing in the street. Who were you trying to impress?"

Carter smiled at Mason. "I like this one."

"Wait till you see her with a knife," he laughed.

"Hella, meet the last Captain, Ed Carter. We just called him the Boss."

"Retirement getting old?"

"Something like that."

"He'll be working with us, but I'm still running the operation."

"Where's Mitchell?"

"He got a little roughed up, Boss. He'll be all right, but he's gonna need another day's rest before we see much of him. I'd love to go on, but we have work to do."

"Shoot."

"Volkov, that's the bastard we're facing, has laid down an ultimatum. We're supposed to be out of this town by something like six hours' time. After that, he says he'll come at us with everything he's got."

"And is that as much as his reputation would have you think?"

"We clipped a good number yesterday, but pretty much, yeah."

"Armour and other vehicles?"

"A few trucks with heavy weapons at least, probably a lot more. Local intel tells us he has five armoured wagons which we haven't seen yet."

Carter shook his head. "You really did land in the shit with this one."

"Yes, so we've got little time to prepare. I'm all ears for any good ideas on how to handle them when they come. My guys reckon he'll come at us in a pincer movement, bringing in his heaviest gear from the north and south roads."

"Sounds about right."

Mason put his datapad down on the table and tapped a few keys until a map of the town was projected on their table.

"We must assume at least something is coming down the eastern road. We're here," he pointed to the bar on the map, slightly east of the central crossroads of the town.

"Vehicle access from only these four roads?"

Mason nodded. It's a simple and compact layout, so pretty much."

"What assets do you have?"

"The team you know, and the new ones you have met, and a good amount of ammunition. Oh, and a tonne of explosives from the mining operation."

"Well, hell, why didn't you say so? Set Archie loose on that kind of gear, and you've got yourself a real party going."

Mason looked down at the map.

"So if we block off the few small access roads, and

funnel them down the main streets, that'll work. Just hope they haven't got V hulls, or our charges ain't gonna do a lot."

"Not likely on a world like this."

"That should take care of the worst of their support, but what about the infantry?"

"How many are we talking, Max?"

"Maybe up to uh...two hundred," his voice dipped when he got to the number.

The Boss' eyes lit up.

"And is any of the town standing with you in this fight?"

"Unlikely. They're miners, tradesmen, and shopkeepers."

"I don't give a high hell what they are. They expect you to fight for them, they better be willing to put something in themselves."

"They are, ten million things."

"Not good enough!"

"All right, so what do you suggest?"

"Least they can do is provide intel throughout. Get comms set up here, and have them in contact at all times. You got some work ahead of you, and not a lot of time to do it. How can you have ever expected to win this fight sitting around waiting for it?"

"We had more than a little trouble yesterday. Mitchell was in deep shit, and we had to do what we had to do to save him."

"Glad to hear it, but that was yesterday, and now it's

today. You need to get moving."

He felt humbled by the Boss, and it was a stark reminder of the man he needed to be.

"Where's the Wizard?"

"He's been across the street all night, Captain." said Erin.

"Doing what?"

"What he needed to do, I hope, getting those explosives ready," Carter said firmly.

Mason got to his feet, and Carter was close behind as they went to investigate. As they left, he called back to Erin.

"Get Hughes set up on the radio, and spotters every three shops in each direction!"

He looked across the street. The door of a mining supplies shop was prised open. He knew it was the place. He and Carter strode and found Archibald at the far end of a counter, obscured by lines of devices he had put together. There was not a single part of the counter top visible.

"Carter, was wondering when you'd turn up."

The Boss looked surprised.

"Oh, come on, biggest fight we've seen in years, and we're to think you wouldn't want a part in it?"

He laughed in response, "Yeah, I figure so."

Mason looked along the counter in astonishment, but he knew he shouldn't have been surprised after working with the Wizard for so long.

"We've got big trouble coming our way. We needed the tools to fight that."

"So what have we got?"

"Ground charges big enough to take out the vehicles we saw yesterday. Trip charges. Have these non-lethal grenades made from a local mineral."

"Non-lethal?"

"Yeah, it's a power which comes close to blinding anyone within maybe three metres. It'll induce vomiting and generally a world of pain."

"Enough to incapacitate?"

"I can't see how it couldn't."

"Good enough."

"What's this?" Carter asked.

He was looking at a large charge that was different to all the others. It stood half a metre tall.

"Well, we haven't seen it yet, but they must have some air transport."

"Be amazed if they didn't," replied Mason.

"Well there's only one roof suitable enough for a landing of anything substantial."

"The med station. Of course, only place in town ever has a reason to come in that way."

"Yep, and you can be sure that bastard knows it," he replied. He got up and paced over to the counter where the device lay. "I call this one the game changer. Med station is just eight shops along. They take it, and we're in trouble."

"Yeah, they secure that landing pad, and they could bypass any of the devices we set on the roads."

"We could blow it?" asked Mason.

"But I think Archie has a more interesting idea in mind, isn't that right?" asked Carter.

"We take out the pad, they change tactics. We blow the pad when they're overhead, and we take out whatever is inside. This is a shaped charge which should maintain the integrity of the roof while taking out anything up to ten or fifteen metres overhead."

"And where does that aircraft go then? Could come down on any of the buildings in the town."

"I said it would work. I didn't say it wasn't dangerous."

Mason smiled. He liked it nonetheless.

"Yes, we can use this."

"We're still missing something though," Carter said.

The two of them looked to him for an answer.

"You said Volkov could have two hundred shooters. Say these devices take out half of those, which would be a big ask, what about the rest?"

"Hey don't look at me," said Andrews. "I can get you this far, rest is up to you."

"When it comes down to it, we're gonna have to slug it out. We have defensive positions, high ground, and a determined will to succeed."

"How do you figure they aren't so motivated?" asked Carter.

"Because ten million credits keeps us in the fight, what about them? And plus, they have somewhere to run when they get scared, where have we got to go?"

"Cornered rats, wonderful."

Mason lifted his comms unit.

"Vik, Liu, start barricading off all routes between the street buildings for as far as you can in the next two hours. Erin, you have those people. Watch and do not let them leave their positions until this is over. Hughes you're on comms in the bar. Hella, you're our only eyes and ears. Everyone get that?"

A string of confirmations came back. He could see the plan was starting to come together, and it was a stark reminder of how unprepared they were that morning. He turned to the Boss who clearly had plenty to say on the matter.

"You think we can do this?" he asked.

"Honestly, I don't know, but we'll give 'em one hell of a fight either way."

Mason nodded in agreement, but deep down he was not at all confident, and the fact the Boss was unsure as he was made him worried.

"Why did you really come back?" he asked Carter.

The Boss took a deep breath and wiped the sweat from his brow. The heat was rising quickly and was a reminder of the brutal temperatures of their last mission.

"You know all these years I looked forward to retirement, and all the peace and easy going life it would entail. Only took me a few days to realise that everything that ever meant anything to me in this life was here, with this crew."

"But you said you'd never have accepted this mission, that it was suicide?"

"Yeah, maybe. But maybe I realised it ain't about just a job, but how we live our lives. I couldn't go and live the easy life knowing my friends still slogged it out for a living."

"Then take back command of the crew and lead us."

He shook his head.

"No, it's time a younger and fitter man had that job. I'm here for you, but you're the Boss."

It was all Mason needed to hear.

"Then let's do this."

CHAPTER TWELVE

"We've got sightings to the east!" Hughes shouted down the comms.

Mason lifted his binoculars to look for confirmation, but he could only see a dust cloud from his position on the roof of the Digger.

"Four vehicles, sounds like what we saw yesterday, plus a quad copter," Hughes continued.

"That'll be the command unit with Volkov."

"That's what I figured, Boss," replied Mason.

"Incoming north and south, six and five respectively," added Hughes.

"Predictable, Boss," said Mason.

"Effective too."

They could see dust clouds where the vehicles were but couldn't make anything out.

"We got a mix of copters and trucks both sides, several

heavily armoured."

"Wizard, confirm you are ready to receive guests?"

"Yeah, I'm ready."

Mason lifted his datapad where he had four camera feeds showing, one from each of the streets leading to the centre of town. The enemy vehicles were closing in rapidly.

"Don't blow them too early."

"I know what I'm doing, Boss."

"North side has passed the waypoint," Hughes reported in.

Mason quickly tapped his screen to bring up the north street only. Two armoured trucks were at the head of the vehicles. They resembled police riot control wagons used on some of the larger worlds. They were covered over with encased gun positions and rifle ports.

"Be a whole world of pain if any of those get through."

"Then let's be sure they don't, Boss."

He lifted up his comms.

"Wizard, be ready on north one."

They watched the screen intently as the vehicles stormed towards them down the empty street.

"South side has passed the waypoint," stated Hughes.

"North one, ready...three, two, fire!" Mason ordered.

A massive explosion erupted which encompassed the lead vehicle and lifted it half a metre off the ground. The camera view was completely clouded in dust for a moment, and the explosion could be felt through their feet. The second truck burst through the smoke.

"North two, fire!" he screamed.

The second explosion was as loud as the first and struck beneath the wheels of the side of the truck, flinging it over onto its side. The upper armour of both looked barely affected, but Mason could see they were crippled, and he doubted anyone could have survived. He quickly turned over to the south view where the column was led by three of the armoured trucks.

"South one, ready? Three, two, fire!"

It blew a whisker early and struck the front of the vehicle, blowing half the armour plating from the engine compartment and ripping the driver compartment apart. It veered wildly out of control and smashed into one of the shops nearby as it went out of camera view. A loud explosion followed as it ignited within the building. The other vehicles behind it ground to a halt before they reached the next devices.

"Shit, that's not good."

"Never expect it to go too smoothly, Max" replied Carter. "That's a hell of a start."

Mason lifted his binoculars to look east and could see Volkov was now standing beside his armoured car.

"So that's him, huh?" Carter asked.

They could both see him giving out new orders.

"He must have called the others to a stop."

"He knows what he's doing, Max."

"Yeah. Way he operates, and the gear he has. I'd say former police force."

"Sounds about right. Well, what do you know? A former cop turned dictator, bullying the locals?"

"If that is the case, he'll quickly change tact."

A few seconds later, they heard a small explosive charge blow to the east in one of the side streets. Mason smiled.

"One of Wizard's trip charges. They must be trying to work their way in through the side alleys. Your move, you son of a bitch."

As the explosion settled, they could hear the sound of engines coming in from the air to the east.

"A transport. Looks too big to land in the streets. Could hold maybe forty guys."

"Just like Andrews reckoned."

"Wizard, be ready on the game changer."

The transport craft came in quickly, and they felt the air and dust engulf them as it swooped in low over the medical station.

"Ready on my go!" yelled Mason.

The transport hovered just two metres over the roof. The rear ramp lowered, and several troops ran to leap from it.

"Now!"

Andrews hit the switch, and the shaped charge blew directly up into the hull and one of the engines of the craft. The engine was torn off by the blast, and the few on the ramp were thrown out onto the roof. It immediately lost power and banked hard, crashing into a building opposite. They knew few if any could have survived the blast and crash together.

"Yeah!" Mason shouted.

He lifted his binoculars to enjoy the look he expected to find on Volkov's face, but the enemy leader showed no emotion at all. He was already busy giving out new orders.

"Look at him, not a care in the world for anyone who works for him."

"And that's why he'll fail, Max. You've broken his assault. Now you must break his army's will to fight."

"Captain, south side is falling back," Hughes said down the line.

Mason looked back to Volkov still reeling off his orders.

"They aren't falling back. What are you up to?"

They watched the screen. Two armoured trucks on the south road appeared to ride out of town.

"I don't like this."

For a few minutes all went silent, but Volkov showed no sign of leaving. Mason lifted his rifle and took aim on the Colonel.

"You'll never hit him from here. Even if you could, you wouldn't get through that armour at this range."

Mason looked up. He knew the Boss was right, but he couldn't resist putting the man in his sights.

"You know this won't be over till he's dead?" asked Mason.

"Sure do."

"Then what's he up to? Because he sure ain't leaving."

Mason scanned the scenery all around them until finally he noticed a dust cloud behind some of the buildings on the other side of the street.

"Look!"

"They're not doing what I think they're doing?"

"Sure are. Liu get out of there, now!" he screamed down his comms.

Ben rushed out of the building towards them when they heard the impact of one of the trucks smashing into the building. He got to the other side of the street as it burst out through the shop front and into the street, with its main laser firing as it came through.

"Down!" he yelled.

Laser fire smashed into the wall before them and launched junks of the solid wall across the roof. They heard another vehicle smash out through the shop the other side of the road and join the fight; a few of their own returned fire.

"This wasn't exactly in the plan!"

He leapt up to the wall, firing a burst down at the vehicle. It returned fire and forced him to duck back down for cover.

"Can't touch it!"

He looked over to see the Boss was grabbing one of Andrews' magnetic charges. It looked like a giant metal disc that was flat on one side and domed the other. He hauled it up from the ground and rushed to the edge to throw it.

"You'll never hit it!"

It was too late. The Boss launched the charge with all his strength, and they both watched as it soared down and clamped onto the roof of one of the vehicles.

"Holy shit!"

Carter didn't have chance to reply. It ignited, and the explosion sent metal fragments rushing towards them. They ducked down just in time to save themselves. Mason looked over to the Boss in shock, but he was staring at Mason. He looked down to see a metal fragment imbedded in the chest section of his armour. It was sticking out thirty centimetres.

"Christ!"

He reached under his armour in a panic to check for blood, but relaxed when he found none.

"Lucky son of a bitch," Carter murmured.

Mason took a hold of the shard of metal, prised it out of his armour, and threw it away across the rooftop. They could hear gunfire still raging below but only one of the heavy weapons. The two of them peeped over the edge and could see the vehicle they struck had been torn apart. The roof was opened like a tin can, and the driver a bloody mess. There was little sign of whoever else may have been inside. Just as soon as they had surveyed the sight, they were being pounded by fire from the heavy laser atop the other truck.

"They're coming in from the east," Hughes called over the comms, "and it sounds like they've got the remains of the northern assault with them."

"Shit, we gotta get that vehicle sorted before they arrive," Mason said to Carter.

"You better be quick then. We've got about a minute or two, if we're lucky."

"Got any ideas?"

"Hey, I just did my part. Next one is yours."

He rushed down the stairs to the next floor and found Liu huddled at the window. Gunfire was smashing through what was left of the windows.

"Whatever you're gonna do, do it fast!" he shouted.

Big help, Mason thought.

"Where's Hell?"

"Last I saw she was in the building across the street with me. Dunno if she made it out, same for Vik!"

He didn't have time to concern himself with her. He carried on down to the next floor, frantically looking around for anything which could help him deal with the armoured truck outside, but the only thing on the bar top was a roll of sticky tape. The gun stopped firing.

Must be reloading. If I don't seize this opportunity, we'll soon be overrun.

He grabbed the tape from the table, drew out a smoke grenade, and launched it out of the main door between him and the vehicle. It was partially covered, but he didn't have time to wait. He pulled a grenade from his webbing, wrapping it in tape as he rushed, keeping low below the smoke. The gun began firing again as he neared it, but it was still firing high up into the bar.

Not gonna die, not gonna die, he told himself.

He reached the vehicle, pushed the tape-covered grenade to the driver's thick armoured glass visor, and quickly jumped underneath the hull. Three seconds later the blast rang out; it was almost deafening. He got to his feet and found the glass had remained intact, but a hole little bigger than his hand had been punched through it. He pulled out one of Wizard's pain grenades, stuffed it through the gap, and then made a run for it. Laser fire followed him as the gunner caught sight, but it stopped immediately as a muted explosion erupted in the vehicle.

He looked back, and a small haze of powder emanated from the hole in the driver's hatch. He could hear coughing and spluttering coming from inside, and it brought him much relief. A few seconds later, a hatch on top of the truck swung open, and the fearsome white powder spewed out into the air and settled over the roof. Mason stood back and held his rifle ready to fire, but they heard whoever was trying to get out slump back down inside the vehicle.

"I guess it was more lethal than he said."

Wizard's voice came over the radio.

"I forgot to mention. In a confined space like that, those grenades can cause unconsciousness or even death."

"Good to know," he replied, realising how serious they could have been had he wanted to use them in a non-lethal capacity. His thought was quickly paused as laser fire struck the ground around him. His instincts got his feet moving, and he was running for the bar as shots landed all around.

He slid in on his ass as the doorway was ripped apart by fire. He got to his feet and rushed behind the bar to where Hughes was set up with all the surveillance gear.

"Tell me what's happening!"

"They've stopped and are mostly out on foot moving through the buildings."

"How many are we talking?"

"Eighty soldiers, easy."

"Shit, we stay here, and we're gonna get our asses blown off."

He lifted up his comms.

"Liu, join me at the rear of the Digger now. Erin, you cover the entrance of the bar. Boss, you keep laying down fire on the roof. Andrews, if you've got anything left, you put it into the street, but be aware we will be among them shortly. Hell? Vik? Where the hell are you?"

There was no response, and he could only assume the two of them were dead or incapacitated at the very least. He heard Liu's footsteps rushing down the stairs.

"Nice job, Captain."

"Yes, but we aren't halfway out of trouble yet."

He stepped through to the bar and saw Erin was hiding behind it, her rifle at the ready.

"If they get here, and they probably will, you're the only one defending that door. You let them through, and Hughes and the Boss could be in trouble. You shoot anyone who comes through that door who isn't one of us, you hear?"

She nodded.

"No bullshit now. I need to know you can do the job. You shoot any bastard you see, then you shoot him again, got that?"

"I got it."

Her voice was a little shaky, but she seemed to be holding it together.

"Relying on you, just as you're relying on us. Keep it together, and we can make it through this."

There was nothing more to be said on the matter. He rushed out to the back of the building with Liu in tow.

"Where we going?"

Mason put his hand out and stopped him, pointing down to one of Wizard's trip wires. Liu breathed out in relief, and they both stepped over it carefully and carried on.

"They think we're holding just the bar. They come at us with everything they've got, and we'll be saturated. Time to mix it up."

"Two against what, fifty?"

"I figure a few more than that."

"And you think we can take 'em?"

"No."

"Great, your confidence is overwhelming."

"You got any grenades left?"

"A few."

"Right then, we're heading for the machine shop a few doors down."

"Why?"

"Because the gear inside gives cover against laser weapons."

"You're the Boss."

"No, I'm the Captain, but I won't be much at all if we fuck this up."

Liu grabbed his arm and stopped him in his tracks.

"Seriously, how are we going to pull this off?"

"I figure we can take at least ten each."

"And the rest?"

"Guess we'll just have to hope for the best. We're here now, and there's nowhere to run, so suck it up, and let's go to work on these assholes."

They reached the machine shop and carefully stepped

over another trip wire to get to the back door, which they figured Wizard had left open as a deliberate attempt at drawing the enemy onto the trap. The interior was filled with heavy machinery, and the frontage was twice as wide as most of the other shops. They took up position a few metres from the front windows they knew would blow out with a single shot.

"Gotta be close now," whispered Liu.

As he said it, a soldier appeared in the window, passing them by.

"Wait, wait, fire."

Three were visible, and they hit them all before they could respond. Glass shattered out across the road and the bodies of those they had killed. Mason rushed to the front, pulling out a grenade as he did. Without putting his head out, he threw the grenade out round the corner towards the east and the rest of the troops approaching. He ducked back down to hear screams as the blast encompassed those who had taken cover from the first shots.

A barrage of gunfire followed, ripping the front of the shop apart and narrowly missing Mason. He ducked back down a few counters away from Liu.

"I think you really pissed them off, Captain!"

"Yeah, well I only just got started."

They could hear the calls of Volkov shouting his orders outside. He was sending troops to the front and rear of the shop.

"He's near now. We're this close to ending it all."

"Yeah, just gotta kill an army to get to him," Liu whispered.

"We don't have to kill them all. We just need to get to him. Kill Volkov, and it ends."

Liu didn't look convinced. Mason wished he could have Hella at his disposal. He could just picture her putting the knife to the Colonel's throat. He wanted to do it himself, but so much of him now desired her training.

They could hear the faint sound of movement all around them and then an explosion. One of Volkov's soldiers had set off the trip wire leading in to the rear of the machine shop. Mason turned to face whoever would come through the dust cloud. Liu still covered the front. The former detective got off the first shots, but it wasn't long before Mason had a soldier appear in his sights. He quickly fired several shots and launched out a grenade past the dead man's body.

"This isn't quite the flanking move I thought you had in mind!"

"It wasn't, Liu!" he shouted back and continued firing.

A grenade was launched through the doorway and pounced up to where Mason was kneeling.

"Grenade!"

The two of them leapt over the wide counters, landing the other side as it blew and rocked the ground. They were deafened by the blast, but the strong structure that had machinery five times the weight of a man on top saved them. The shop lit up as Liu fired out towards the shattered windows, but neither of them could hear anything. Calls were coming through on his comms, but he couldn't hear them and continued dealing with the enemy before him.

Laser pulses raced through the shop between them, and they returned as much fire. After thirty seconds, Mason's hearing began to return, and he could just make out frantic calls over the comms.

"We're overrun, overrun, need help in here!"

He could just make out that it was Hughes' voice, and he heard a few shots before the line went quiet. His hearing was getting better, but his head was throbbing with pain from the explosion. He turned to Liu. He was firing as quickly as he could to keep the enemy at bay.

"Bar is in trouble!"

"You go. I got this," replied Liu confidently.

He hated the idea of leaving his friend behind, but he knew so many more friends were in danger. His confidence in Liu was all that got him to his feet and moving for the door. Another shooter rushed through the rear entrance, with his rifle to fire. He got off the first shot, and it hit Mason's body armour, but he weathered it and kept firing. Three shots struck the shooter and killed him. He had to step over several bodies to reach the door and found more outside. Only one man remained, and he put down his weapon when Mason reached the doorway.

"Go on, get!" Mason yelled.

The man ran for his life as the Captain stepped through the scattered bodies of those who had attacked them. He rushed for the back of the bar without checking a thing. It was risky, but he knew time was of the essence. Hughes was at his console and nursing a wound from a shot that had struck his body between his armour and his shoulder. He was unable to stand, held a pistol in his hand, but wasn't even able to lift it.

"Where?" Mason asked.

"The roof," he replied, though obviously in pain.

"You hold on. We'll get through this!"

Hughes just about lifted his pistol, and to Mason's surprise, loosed off a shot. One of the shooters dropped dead beside him. He nodded in gratitude and headed out quickly to the front. The silhouette of an enemy soldier was coming through the front door. He was surprised to meet the barrel of Mason's gun and several shots knocking him out the door. Three bodies lay at the entrance, beside the one he had just shot. He knew Erin had shot them.

She's done her part, and that gives me hope.

He looked out to see dozens of shooters approaching from the east. Just when the situation seemed hopeless, he heard the coarse growly voice of Viktor across the road.

"Come on, you fuckers!"

It was followed by a hail of gunfire from a heavy

weapon the hulking man had ripped from the roof of one of the trucks they had disabled earlier. Blood poured from his mouth, and he was almost entirely covered in dust and dirt, but he was back in the fight. It spurred Mason on, and he turned and rushed for the roof. As he got to the last flight of stairs, he heard a shot ring out and a scream follow it.

At the top of the stairs, Mason found the Boss. He was bleeding out at the neck. Bodies of the enemy shooters surrounded him, and Volkov held Erin hostage. Mason rushed to the Boss, dragged him back out of view and applied pressure, but he was fading fast. With his last energy, he smiled and said, "Kill that bastard!"

A single tear dropped from one of Mason's eyes as he realised he'd lost his oldest friend and father figure in a split second. It was too much to handle right then, so he turned his attention away for follow the Boss' final request. It was far from the ending Mason had ever wished for him, but it was not the time to dwell on it. He pulled out the magazine on his rifle. It was empty.

I never cared for rifles anyway. You're gonna die, you son of a bitch!

He stepped out with his hand close to his holstered gun. Volkov's expression was still confident and loathing. He held a pistol to Erin's head. Mason could see the fear in her eyes. More than anything else she didn't want to die.

"It's over Volkov!"

"Really? Because it looks like you haven't got much left to stand on. I kill this one, and you're another one down. Not many left standing."

"Or I could shoot you in the head right here and now, and it's all over."

"No, your girlfriend here means too much to you for that."

Mason wanted nothing more than to draw out his pistol and fire, but he couldn't risk it. They both heard engines roar as something drew near. He saw Volkov take a quick look and turned back with a broader smile. He threw Erin forward, and she stumbled towards Mason. He caught her and watched Volkov leap from the rooftop. He rushed to the edge and could see he had jumped onto one of his quad copters and was already fifty metres away. Mason fired two shots, but they didn't even come close to hitting him.

"Fuck!" he screamed.

CHAPTER THIRTEEN

Mason stood over the body of the Boss. He'd had him laid out on a table downstairs. He never thought he'd see the day the Boss died, not even from old age. Erin and Andrews struggled with Hughes to get him over to one of the tables. Hughes was wincing in pain and was no longer able to use a crutch to support his legs, due to the chest injury. Mason shook his head and turned to the door, looking out at the carnage.

One of the armoured trucks was still burning from the charge the Boss had thrown on it, and bodies were strewn all around. He heard a loud crack. Across the street, a boot connected with a door that was barely held on. Vik had kicked it open, and it fell from its hinges. He stepped out with Hella in his arms. She was barely conscious and covered in as much grey soot and dust as he was. Blood poured from a head wound of Vik, but he did his best not to show the pain. He carried Hell's weight like she was a child.

"How is she?" asked Mason.

"Alive."

He stepped through into the bar and found one of the few tables still standing and placed her down carefully. She was rambling and not yet lucid.

"Building came down on our heads. Fucker's drove right through the ground floor. It just gave way."

"I know," Mason replied softly.

Vik looked surprised to see the other two casualties. They both heard a few shots ring out outside, and they knew it was Liu finishing off the enemy dead. It wasn't that he enjoyed it. He just liked to tie up loose ends. Mason was astonished to see Vik stroll over to Hughes and stand over him, resting a hand on his good shoulder in concern.

"You okay?" he asked.

Hughes was as surprised as Mason, and it was enough to make him forget the pain for a second as Andrews cut and removed his clothing to get to the wound. Erin sat down and was in shock over what had happened. She couldn't stop staring at the body of the Boss.

"Is this over?" she asked.

Mason turned to her, and the others stopped to listen.

"Not a chance. Volkov is going down."

"How, what have we got left?"

"We've got each other, Erin. We were paid to put an

end to this, and that's exactly what we'll do."

"With what?" Andrews asked. "Boss is gone. Hughes ain't going anywhere. Hella looks like she might come around with a few days' rest."

"I don't care. You take care of them. Rest of you, gather your ammunition and be ready to move in five."

Andrews strode over and led him out of the bar through the ruins of the entrance.

"Look at it," he said, pointing at the carnage. "Haven't you done enough?"

"No, Volkov has to die. You do your job, and we'll do ours."

He stepped back into the bar to address the others.

"How we gonna do this?" asked Liu. He'd just come through from the back of the bar. "Volkov must have quite a place. Can't imagine we'd get through with Mily."

"The Boss' new ship. We'll ram it down his throat."

"And then?"

"Then we kill everyone in sight," Viktor replied.

Mason nodded in agreement. He was liking the plan more and more.

"All the planning we've done for ops, and that's your plan?"

"I'm done planning, Liu. Volkov dies today."

There was no more room for discussion. Just ten minutes later they were aboard the Boss' ship and lifting off. Andrews watched them from what was left of the entrance of the Digger, as they soared off east towards the Colonel's compound. He caught movement out of the corner of his eye. It was Kaper stumbling towards him, open mouthed in shock. He was close to tears as he looked at the carnage of the bar. Half the sign was gone, most of the windows were blown out, and the door barely clung to the building.

"What happened? Did we win?"

Andrews shook his head.

"Not yet, but you can be sure this will end today. Now come inside. We have casualties, and I need your help."

Mason was at the control of the ship. It was a lavish vessel, the likes of which he'd rarely ever seen up close. There was almost nothing inside the ship to identify it as Carter's, just a single photo of the team from five years before.

"It really was all that mattered to him? This team?"

"What else should matter, Erin? We're in this life together. The Boss realised he didn't want to give up this life, and why should he?"

"So he died happy?"

Mason nodded in agreement, and Erin was starting to understand it was a good death.

"Volkov must know we're coming. He'll see us coming a mile off."

He won't see this coming, Liu."

The ship soared towards Volkov's luxury mansion with

lightning speed. As they approached, they could see on their display it was a walled residence, and many of the survivors of the fight in town were still unloading from their vehicles.

"No, you're not doing what I think you're doing?" asked Liu.

"Hell, yes!"

The complex was four storeys high and lavish in size. It was of square construction with a centrally enclosed courtyard and walled gates out front. Several of the enemy soldiers looked up in amazement as the ship soared towards them. A couple took shots, but it was too late. Carter's ship smashed into the wall of the compound and burst through three rooms and out into the courtyard. It was propelled into the far sidewall and struck through into the second storey. It was on the opposite side to where most of Volkov's troops were stationed.

They rocked to a halt. Mason was first on his feet to open the ramp. The mechanism was slightly jammed. He kicked it, but it didn't budge.

"Allow me!" Vik scowled.

Mason barely managed to get out of the way as he launched himself at the ramp. It burst open, and Viktor tumbled out into the wreckage and debris they had left behind. They leapt out behind him; acutely aware they were just four fighters in the lion's den.

"Let's get this fucker," stated Mason. They advanced

towards the nearest door and could hear the cries of panic from those inside. Mason hit the door switch, and the double doors quickly slid open. Three shooters were approaching, and Erin was first to fire. Her accurate shot caught the man in the middle of the face and killed him outright. The other two were riddled by bursts from Mason and Viktor.

"You got a plan?" asked Liu.

"Kill them all," he replied sternly.

They were inside a large dining room fit for forty guests, and passed either side of the table. Every element of the building was decadently decorated so that Volkov could live like a King.

"Guess we know where his money's been going," Liu said.

They passed into the next corridor and found a guard frantically trying to tap in a key code of a door that was clearly an important room. Viktor shot out his legs with two shots, and he dropped hard to the ground. Mason was on him before he could get his pistol from his holster, grabbed him by the collar of his shirt, and lifted his torso so he winced in pain from the pressure on his legs.

"What's in the room?" he yelled.

The man shook his head as if to say no, but he was scared to death.

Mason put his rifle down and drew his knife. He first lifted it to the man's throat, but it didn't seem to get the response he wanted. He put the knife to the man's groin and pressed just slightly.

"The code or your balls!"

"31675, 31675," he quickly stated.

"Now there's the Captain I can follow," Viktor said, smiling.

Mason reversed the blade and smashed the pommel down on the man's face, knocking him out cold.

"What if he lied about the code?"

"Erin, he gave us everything he had to give, trust me."

Mason punched in the code, and the door slid open. It was twenty centimetres thick and heavily reinforced. What lay inside brought a glint to their eyes.

"It's Volkov's armoury."

"Well how about that, Liu," said Mason.

"You just struck gold," Vik said, rushing inside like a kid in a toyshop. Mason reached for a large box magazine fed scatter laser shotgun. It was the kind of weapon rarely suited to the kind of work they did, but when maximum carnage at close range was the order of the day, it was the gun to have.

"Gather what you need, and let's go."

Viktor took an M41 heavy laser, a sustained fire weapon usually used with a bipod, but he was strong enough to wield it at the hip. They rushed out of the room and hit the door switch behind them. Mason smashed the rifle of his shotgun into the keypad, and it fizzled with sparks before going dead. Footsteps were approaching fast and in large numbers.

"They must be coming for gear."

"Then they probably don't know we're here, Liu."

They lifted their weapons to the doorway. As it swung open, they saw the surprise on the faces of the four soldiers before them. Mason opened up on full auto with his shotgun, and the two in the middle were torn apart. The other two didn't last much longer once Viktor had started firing.

Mason noticed movement off to their side, and he turned in time to see Hunter freeze as he recognised him. He drew his pistol and fired, but was quickly pushed back behind cover when Mason's shotgun opened fire. The others were about to join in when lasers started to rush over the bodies of the enemy towards them, forcing them to cover also.

"Go for Hunter. We'll hold here!" said Liu.

"Give him a good kicking for me!" Viktor shouted.

Mason leapt out from cover and rushed towards Hunter's position; his weapon firing to keep the Sergeant down. He reached the point where he had last seen him. There was movement up ahead, and he caught sight of him falling back further. He rushed on to catch up. Common sense and training told him he shouldn't, but after Volkov, Hunter was one who needed to pay.

He took a bend and found a pistol pointed at his head.

He ducked just in time for the blast to skim the armour of his shoulder. Mason lifted his gun to fire, but it was kicked out of his hands. He jumped up and grabbed Hunter's pistol, ducked under his arm, and prised it up almost taking the man's arm out of its socket. He dropped the pistol but delivered two quick kidney punches that knocked Mason back.

As he got his footing, Mason quickly drew his pistol and fired twice from the hip, but Hunter was already behind cover.

"Come out you, bastard!"

"Why, so you can shoot me where I stand?"

"Sounds pretty good to me!"

Mason approached the position where he had just fired and found nothing. A shot skimmed near by his body, and he turned quickly, seeing one of the shooters down the corridor. He responded with two quick shots and killed the man, but before he could turn back, Hunter was on him. He struck him hard with a kick to the ribs and an uppercut to the face. It launched him back and the pistol from his hands. Blood spewed from his mouth as he got back to his feet.

"Ready for another beating, Captain?"

"How can you work for Volkov? He's an asshole."

"A rich asshole. How can I work for him? Look at this place! To work for the Colonel is to have everything you ever wanted."

"At the price of extorting everyone decent around you?"

"Tell it to someone who gives a shit."

He lunged forward with a jab. Mason avoided it and struck back with a hook, just clipping the Sergeant. He followed it up with a hard hook to his stomach and went for another when the Sergeant locked his elbow and flipped him over onto his back. Mason rolled over and quickly got back to his feet, but Hunter came at him relentlessly. He delivered a barrage of punches until he got a clinch and threw Mason over.

The wind was taken out of the Captain as he landed. As he recovered, he found Hunter stood over him with his own gun in his face.

"Game over, Captain."

As he was about to squeeze the trigger, Viktor's Griswold flew into view and struck Hunter in the face. The heavy lump of a pistol had been thrown from ten metres away and hit like a hammer. Hunter stumbled a few steps and dropped Mason's gun. Viktor strode into view with machine gun in hand. He reached down and hauled Mason to his feet.

"I'll take this punk. You get Volkov."

Mason was glad of the help, and his hulking friend looked all too keen to take over. He dropped his machine gun to the floor and gestured for Hunter to come forward. Hunter still looked confident, but as they closed, he realised the size of Viktor.

"I'm gonna enjoy this."

Mason nodded in appreciation, holstered his pistol, and picked up his shotgun.

"Don't go easy on him now."

"No worry of that."

Mason rushed onwards to find the man he really wanted to kill. He came to a stairway where a group of the militia were running up to join the fight. He ran to the top and opened up on full auto. The first man was blow apart by the first two shots. The rest smashed into his comrades; bodies and wounded collapsed down the stairway on top of those below.

* * *

Hunter kicked high, but Viktor took the kick and got a hold of his leg. He launched Hunter across the room, and he tumbled into a wall. He got back to his feet and rushed forward. Viktor threw a heavy hook that Hunter ducked under and drove a knee hard up into Viktor's stomach, forcing him to keel over slightly. But he recovered quickly and took a hold of Hunter's legs and pulled. He crashed to the ground face first. Hunter spun and kicked Vik's legs out from under him so that they were both flat on the floor.

Viktor rolled over and struck with a backfist, knelt

over Hunter and punched him repeatedly to the head. He stopped half the strikes but was still taking a barrage that he couldn't last long against. He kicked up, catching Viktor to the temple with his heavy combat boots. Viktor was knocked back and rolled over, getting to his feet with a stagger.

"When fighters like you stay home and rob the locals, it's no wonder the Alliance is losing the war."

Hunter looked down at the belt that identified Viktor. Looking at the pistol across the floor that had struck him, confirmed it.

"You aren't exactly out fighting the cause either," he spat back.

"Maybe I prefer killing punks like you."

Viktor roared as he rushed forward with the assault.

* * *

"Run!" Liu screamed.

Erin raced to where they were falling back, and he threw a grenade around the corner where she had come from. It exploded and was followed by screams of pain by those caught in the blast.

"Keep moving!"

Erin struggled to reload her rifle as they made their way to the next line of cover.

"Where are we going?"

"Anywhere, so as not to get overrun!"

He turned and took a knee beside the frame of an archway leading into a conference hall.

"We can't keep running forever."

"Then nail these next bastards, and let's see if we can't hold some ground."

The militia continued to advance, but the first two were cut down by fire. The next few fired as they came through, but the shots didn't find their targets, as both Erin and Liu fired from cover. As another of the militiamen was struck down, the other two grabbed him and hauled him back to safety.

"All right, they're starting to lose momentum."

* * *

Mason's gun raged as he stepped through into a hallway where militiamen were gathering up ammunition from a table. He was firing on full auto, and blood spewed out over the counter when only one managed to return fire. The shot hit the gun and hit into his armour. He jolted slightly, the broken shotgun falling from his hands. He ripped his pistol out and fired two shots from the hip, killing the man instantly.

A stairway led up beyond their position to an elevated luxury office space. He could already tell it must be Volkov's centre of operations.

"Volkov! I'm coming for you!" he roared at the top of his voice.

He heard a weapon cock inside the large room. He rushed up the steps without any form of caution.

I want blood, and I want it soon!

The entrance was completely round, leading to a wide hallway that opened out into a bar with sofas and large projection screens. It was more like a playboy's mansion than a Colonel's office.

"Volkov! Come out and fight me, you coward!"

His voice came over speakers all around the room.

"What is it you want from me, Captain? What? Money? Power? Do you want to be my new right hand and share in this wealth?"

"I want your head!"

It all went quiet. Mason expected to see the Colonel coming at him at any moment and turned continually with his pistol held at the ready. Instead, he was greeted by the sound of machinery firing up and doors opening high on the walls. He looked up at robotically mounted lasers articulating out from the walls. Looking back for just a second, he could see even heavier weapons at the entrance.

"Oh, shit."

He launched into a running pace further into the room as laser fire landed at his feet. One of them scorched his shoe, and he leapt over a large conference table for cover.

He breathed heavily, looking around for a way out. The guns had stopped firing. He was safe for a moment.

"What is your price, Mason?" Volkov asked over the tannoy.

The fact he's asking means he's scared.

Gunfire still raged throughout the building. Volkov had no idea how many Mason had with him, and it was better it stayed that way.

"I'm not going to let you live, Mason. Keep this up, maybe you'll kill me, maybe you won't, but what about the price to you and your friends? How many more of them have to die before you call it enough?"

"You're really starting to bore me!"

"Then let me make your life more interesting, Captain."

Ah, shit, I'm not gonna like this!

Doors opened in the ceiling above him. He looked up, and clamps were coming off a domed device half a metre wide. He jumped to his feet and ran as fast as he could as the dome dropped. As it reached the middle of the room, it erupted with a white flash of light and a blast, propelling Mason through the air. It slammed him into the far sidewall.

He just about got to his feet when a ten-metre radius around where he had previously stood had been vaporised. He tried to shake of the ringing in his ears and was just about getting his hearing back.

"I'm still standing, you bastard!"

He took pleasure in knowing Volkov was probably cursing the gods as he stood defiantly before the damage. He looked around. He was now standing beside a large ornate desk with a comfy chair behind it and a drinks cabinet at the side.

"So this is your throne? Doesn't look like much, anymore."

He scanned the area, trying to find any sign of where the Colonel could be hiding, and then he saw it; a safe room door. A display cabinet obscured it, but the blast had revealed the frame.

"Hiding like the coward you are?"

No response came.

"Unfortunately for you, Colonel, this ain't the first time I've had to deal with a safe room." He walked along the edge of the wall, tapping it with his pistol butt.

"Pretty much every one builds the air filtration system into the wall."

His pistol tapped a hollow point. "And there you have it."

He turned his pistol around and fired three shots into the area. The interior wall fragmented. He pulled the last grenade from his vest and looked up to the door for one last moment.

"Last chance, Colonel."

No reply came. He twisted the arming cap and stuffed the grenade in through the hole until it hit the metalwork of the air cleaner. He quickly rushed back and hid behind the heavy-duty desk as the explosion blew the room apart. Smoke clouded the office as he rushed to the blast area. The grenade had blown the filtration system apart, creating a hole big enough to crawl through. He peered in. It was just a few metres square inside, and there was an open door the other side.

"Goddamn it."

He crawled through into the space. Volkov couldn't have been inside when the grenade erupted. Shards of the filtration system were imbedded like shrapnel in all four walls, and yet there was no sign of blood.

"Gonna have to flush you out," he said to himself.

* * *

Erin reloaded her rifle and looked out down the corridor. It was eerily quiet.

"Where are they, Liu?" she asked.

"Maybe they've run?" he answered hopefully.

She shook her head, turning back to see a fresh wave rush through the door, screaming as they fired.

"No such luck!"

They fired back, but as they did, Erin heard a laser fire from behind them. Liu dropped to the floor, and smoke poured from his body armour where he had been struck. One of the militiamen turned the bend at their side, and she hit him with the stock of her rifle as hard as she could. It stopped him in his tracks and knocked him back a little, enough that she could turn the rifle around and fire two shots into his chest.

She looked back; Liu was still firing at the rest.

Thank God for body armour, he thought.

None of the militiamen wore the expensive ballistic armour they did, a fact that spoke volumes of their leader.

"We can't hold like this much longer!"

"Just keep firing, Erin. They haven't got infinite numbers. Many more, and they'll break!"

She looked down at the trail of bodies leading up to their position.

"When?" she asked.

They kept up the fire as lasers still shot past their heads. Erin's rifle ran out, and she reached for the dead militiaman's beside her. It was a bulky weapon compared to the one Mason had given her, but it was better than nothing.

"Give it up!" Liu shouted. "Your Colonel doesn't care for your lives! Don't die for nothing!"

They both knew the militiamen kept fighting because they were being paid handsomely to do so, and it was hard to beat that. Liu was praying Mason had found Volkov and was dealing with him, for if not, they were in serious trouble.

CHAPTER FOURTEEN

"Come on!" Viktor roared.

Hunter was looking tired and blood gushed from both his mouth and nose, but Viktor's face was swelling up from strikes too, and they were both beginning to slow. Vik's smile weighed heavily on Hunter psychologically - he couldn't break his opponent. Viktor wasn't much of a technical fighter or one who would put on much of a pretty display, but he was a veteran brawler.

The Sergeant quickly jabbed twice at Viktor who took the punches and answered them with a hard hook that Hunter was too tired to avoid. He staggered back from the strike but came right back at him with a kick to the inside of Viktor's knee. It wobbled his leg slightly. Hunter continued forward to press the advantage and drove in with a knee. It never connected; Viktor struck him hard with a straight punch that threw his upper body back while his legs still went forward. He slammed hard into the ground, but Viktor wasn't done with him.

He grabbed the Sergeant by the collar and hauled him to his feet. Hunter tried to punch to the ribs but was met with a headbutt to the face. It burst his already bleeding nose. Viktor stepped forward, grabbed Hunter, rotated him fully, and dropped him on his head. The Sergeant's neck snapped as he hit the floor, and his body went limp. Viktor let go, allowing it to slump down in front of him.

Vik wiped the sweat and blood from his face and then smiled in response. It was the most fun he'd had all day, but a relief having won.

* * *

Volkov was running down the corridors of his ruined palace, hoping to find any of his militia.

"Hunter?" he whispered. "Sergeant Hunter?"

He called but no response came.

"Fuck, fuck," he said quietly to himself. He heard gunfire and turned to look down a long room and smiled. He thought he'd found allies and got moving, only to stop dead as he saw Erin and Liu fighting frantically. He turned back to change direction but had the shock of his life to find Mason standing before him.

"No where left to run, Colonel."

Volkov saw Mason's hands were empty. The only gun

he had was holstered at his side. He smiled as he took a firmer grip on the multi-laser he was carrying.

"You're a little outgunned, don't you think?"

"Size isn't everything. You know how to use yours?"

Volkov took his opportunity and lifted the weapon to fire, but Mason's gun was out of the holster and lighting up the room before he could even take aim. Volkov yelped as a shot hit his gun and burnt the back of his right hand. The gun fell from his hands.

"Fuck!" he screamed, spinning around in pain. "What are we even doing this for? I offered you everything you could have ever dreamed of!"

"You've taken what can never be replaced."

"And you've killed too. Let's not forget who started the killing?"

"Tell it to someone who cares."

"What are they paying you for this job? Twenty?"

"Ten."

Volkov laughed.

"Ten? I'll give you twenty just to walk out of here and leave this world."

"A nice offer, but you see, here's the problem. I took a job, and I'm gonna finish it."

Volkov shook his head and then flicked his wrist. A small pocket gun slid out from his sleeve. He fired before Mason noticed what was going on. The shot hit his right arm, forcing him to release the grip on his pistol. As the second shot came at his head, he ducked and rolled forward, launching him into Volkov. He knocked them both to the floor.

Mason reached down and took a hold of the gun and its fragile fixing, ripped it from his wrist, and threw it aside. His right arm felt weak, but he was ignoring it with all his strength. Volkov had drawn Mason's knife and thrust it towards him. He got a lock on his wrist in time, striking him twice in the head to make him loosen his grip. The Captain got up and threw the knife aside.

"Every cheap play in the book. You're no man. You're pathetic," Mason sneered.

He let Volkov get to his feet and take a stance. Although he was certainly trained, Mason didn't care.

"Why not take the money? Retire, buy a place like this, and live how you want to live?" he asked.

"Time for talk is over. It's time for you to answer for what you have done."

"And you think you are the man to do it?"

He rushed forward, driving a surprisingly quick snap kick into Mason's stomach and a knee into the side of his head. Mason stumbled across the room, gathering his composure.

"Good, I thought this was gonna be too easy."

Volkov came at him once against, first with a punch. Mason got a lock on it, collapsed his elbow in at the joint, and drove a hard knee into his abdomen. He recovered quickly and spun out of the lock, kicked Mason's knee out from behind, and took a chokehold. It was a hard hold, and Mason was already starting to feel the air being restricted. He reached back to punch Volkov in the head but couldn't get any power into the strike.

Mason's vision was starting to blur, and he could feel the energy being sapped out his body.

No way, he told himself.

He drove his elbow into Volkov's side twice. It didn't force him to release his grip but was enough to gain some room to manoeuvre. He stamped down on Volkov's foot with all the strength he could muster and crushed his toes. Through the pain, his grip weakened slightly. Mason reached back, took a hold of his hair, and yanked him overhead. He was thrown over Mason's shoulder and crashed down onto the floor.

The wind was blasted out of Volkov's lungs, but Mason went down on one knee and took some deep breaths. He watched as Volkov got to his feet and tried to run towards a stairway. Mason staggered to his feet and rushed after the Colonel. He reached him as he got to the top of the stairs and barged into him. They both crashed through a large window at the top of the stairs.

They burst out from the first floor window of the inner courtyard and were showered in glass. Mason had only a second to see what they were heading for, an open swimming pool. They crashed into the water, narrowly missing the hard edges that would have split their skulls open.

Volkov was up first, wading through the water to the shallow ramp to get out, but Mason was close behind. He leapt forward, managing to catch the back of his shirt and drag them both under. Volkov turned and fought back with a flurry of shots as they re-surfaced, but Mason blocked the first two, hitting with a straight punch and immediately following with an elbow. The impact landed hard and stunned the Colonel.

Mason grabbed a hold of his head before he could recover and smashed it down on the edge of the pool. He immediately pulled it back and did the same again. Volkov's head split open and blood gushed out into the water. A third time made sure, and Mason let go. Volkov's body floated out across the water. Blood continued to spread out all around the two of them.

He looked up. Erin was standing at a doorway ten metres in front of him and looking in horror. He thought she was appalled by the brutality, but the next words out of her mouth surprised him.

"You okay?"

He nodded in agreement and strode up the ramp, the bloody water dripping from him. Footsteps approached from the opposite side to Erin. Mason watched as half a dozen militiamen appear at the doorway. They stopped, looking in shock at the blood filled pool and floating body of their leader. Mason glared at them with murderous intent, but he also knew unarmed he was in trouble if they were to keep fighting.

"It's over. Go home," he stated.

They were still stunned and uncertain of what to do.

"You heard the man!" yelled Viktor.

He appeared at a first floor window, opposite the one the Captain had fallen from. Viktor held the massive gun he had taken from the armoury and looked all too happy for the opportunity to use it. Mason looked back at the soldiers and could already hear the sound of their guns touching the ground. They hurriedly left without another word.

"They were gonna surrender to me!" Mason shouted.

"Yeah, when a man's got a gun trained on me, I'd rather be sure. They just needed a little convincing."

Liu hobbled in and stood by Erin.

"You finish it?" he asked before he could see the evidence for himself.

"Little dramatic, don't you think?" he asked, looking at the blood pool.

Mason sighed in relief, "It's over."

"Shame, it was starting to get fun," added Viktor.

"What now?" asked Erin.

"We collect our payment."

* * *

They rolled back into town in Volkov's personal wagon. It had comfy seats and a great air conditioning system, but the mirrored windows meant nobody could see inside as they came in from the east. Many of the town's people were out and had already begun the clean up. Most stopped and stared at the vehicle. They reached the bar, and Mitchell was on guard. He had a table set up with a heavy weapon resting on the table. He took careful aim at their approach. The doors opened, and he dropped the stock of the weapon and smiled.

"Holy shit."

He got up to greet them but was still a little unsteady on his feet. Viktor helped Liu out and dragged him along with little effort at all.

"They're back!"

The others came out to greet them. Andrews supported Hughes, and Hella looked like she was recovering from the world's worst hang over.

"You kill him?"

"Damn straight, Hell!"

"So it's over?" asked Hughes.

He looked around the town and the bodies and debris still strewn about.

"For us, yes. But there's one more thing we have to do."

Fifteen minutes later, they were riding out of town with the Boss' body for burial. None of the town's folk were with them, but they were happy to keep it to their crew only.

"Where'd you want to do this?" Liu asked.

Mason looked around and saw a lone tree, the only significant feature of the landscape.

"There." He turned the copter.

"Think he'd want it this way?"

"I don't think he'd care much how we do it, only that we're here for his send off."

The tone was unsurprisingly sombre as they drew up to the tree.

"You know what to do," said Mason.

He, Liu, and Vik grabbed shovels and started digging. They could have used machinery from the town to do it, but it felt impersonal. It took a solid hour of sweating to dig up the dry ground before they could finally lay his body to rest. They covered the grave back over until it was barely noticeable the ground had ever changed.

"No gravestone?"

"He wouldn't care for it, Erin."

Mason took up position in front of the grave to say a last few words.

"Ed Carter, the Boss. Best man I ever knew. Took me in, taught me to be what I am today. Most importantly, he was there when we needed him. He died just as he lived, fighting for us all."

Nobody else had a word to say as they reflected on his death. The stood silently for a few minutes, and finally turned back to the vehicles.

"What now?" asked Erin.

"Andrews is making the last few repairs to the Lady, and we're out of here."

"Just like that?"

"Just like that. But not before they deliver payment."

They rode back to the ship and found a few dozen people from the town waiting for them. Nolan Machesky was at the head and Kaper just to his side. He carried a case they knew would be full of the money they had fought hard to earn. Mason stepped up to collect.

"I want to thank you for all you have done."

"We destroyed your town."

"No, it was already falling apart. Whatever damage was done today can be fixed with half the money Volkov was stealing from us in a month."

He passed over the case of money. Mason thought for a moment of giving some of it back, but then he was reminded of the hardships they had faced to get it. He took it with a smile, handed it to Liu to take care of.

"I can't say I want to come back here anytime soon, but I wish you every luck."

"We're free to go about our lives as we always wanted, Captain, like you do. Good luck and safe journey."

Mason nodded and looked up at the ship. It was still partly imbedded in the dusty surface from when they made their emergency landing.

"Yeah, I hope so."

The locals passed through them and shook their hands. They climbed into their vehicles, returning to get on with rebuilding their town.

"I'm gonna miss this place," Viktor said.

They all looked at him to clarify his meaning.

"Really?" asked Hughes.

"No," he quickly replied.

They laughed, and it was a welcome break and return to the status quo.

"Seems a shame to leave that truck," said Viktor, pointing to Volkov's luxury armoured vehicle.

"If you want to settle here and keep it, you're more than welcome, but that shit stays off my boat," Mason said sternly.

He lifted up his comms unit. "Andrews, how much longer?"

"Should be about ready."

Mason looked to Mitchell.

"I'm on it."

He rushed up the ramp towards the cockpit.

"With any luck, we're getting outta here. Liu, get Mily loaded up. Let's go."

A minute later, the engines pulsated and fired up to cheers from most of the crew. Mason looked down the ramp for one last time when he noticed a dust cloud with a single vehicle approaching. It was a Marshals' copter. He waited for them to disembark. They stepped up towards the ramp to address him. Three men came forward in a scene reminiscent of the last time they failed.

"Captain Mason?"

"Who's asking?"

"Deputy Willows. I have a warrant for the arrest of Captain Max Mason and crew for murder, attempted murder, trespassing, and quite frankly, a whole host of other offences. Are you Captain Mason?"

"I think you already know that, son."

"Then come peacefully. You are to stand trial before an Alliance court for your crimes."

Mason smiled and turned around to the others. Liu stood beside him, and he noticed one of Andrew's pain grenades in his webbing. He lifted up his comms unit.

"Mitchell, prepare for lift off in five."

He turned around, grabbed hold of the grenade as he did, twisted the arming cap, and lobbed it into the middle of them. The engines roared, and the ship lifted off as the grenade ignited. The three men disappeared into a cloud of white dust. Mason could hear them coughing and screaming as they gained altitude, and he hit the door ramp button.

"Didn't anybody tell 'em not to play with fire?" Liu grinned.

He turned around. The others were waiting for his word now they were finally on their way.

"Nice work, all of you. As always, I have a line on a few jobs. But for now, we've got ten million credits to spend and nowhere we need to be."

Liu pulled out beers from a crate and tossed them out. They clashed them together.

"To the Boss, to us, and to making money!" said Mason.

Liu looked around the room at the rag tagged group of mercenaries they had assembled and smiled. They had become a family in the short time they had worked together. He lifted up his beer.

"To Mason's Maniacs!"